Detroit Muscle

Jeff Vande Zande

WHISTLING SHADE
PRESS

St. Paul MN
www.whistlingshade.com

First Edition, First Printing
April 2016

Excerpts from *Detroit Muscle* appeared in the following venues:
Bibliotekos
Squalorly
Midwestern Gothic

ISBN 978-0-9829335-6-5

Book design by Joel Van Valin

Cover design by Jennifer Barko
Cover photo by Tony Detroit

Printed in the United States of America

This novel is dedicated to my mother,
Elaine Vande Zande, a former substance
abuse counselor, and the tough muscle
that always kept our family going…

"The only thing separating Detroit from the rest of Michigan is a comma. As Detroit goes, so goes Michigan."

—Former Michigan State Senate Majority Leader Randy Richardville

"You are a hymnal too, I said aloud to myself.
A scrap metal mantra. Beauty inside rust."
—Ken Meisel, "Detroit Hymnal"

"Muscles actually have a memory of their former strength—and that memory may last indefinitely."

—Kristian Gundersen, University of Oslo

Below, Detroit sprawls outward in asphalt and cement, juts upward in brick and glass, from the bank of its namesake river. A rust-colored freighter sits suspended on the waterway crossing under the Ambassador Bridge. In the near urban distance, the white-roofed Ford Field and the green diamond of Comerica Park sit side by side. The seven skyscrapers of the Renaissance Center tower over the water. Overlooking the financial district, the stately Detroit One Center. The Greater Penobscot Building. The Guardian Building. Minoru Yamasaki's One Woodward Avenue building, the design of which he would borrow from to create the World Trade Center. On the ground, a twisting of interstate and highways merge into the grid of city streets hosting a rat race of cars.

It is a masquerade. A charade. A smokescreen.

Down there too, in more abundance, pockets of desolation and loss spread horizontally across the urban landscape. The Packard Motor Plant. Fisher Body Plant 21. Detroit Gray Iron. AMC Headquarters. Peerless Cement. Roberts Brass Works. Grand Trunk Cold Storage. Thorn Apple Valley Slaughterhouse. The abandon spreads, including the nameless rotting rec centers, golf courses, playgrounds, stadiums, and community centers. The city's vertical reach is also an illusion. Entire buildings stand abandoned. The 15 floors of Charles Noble's Art Deco Lee Plaza. The gigantic Michigan Central Station. The 38 floors of Book Tower on Washington Boulevard. The Free Press Building. Too many vacant buildings to name. A city of empty stories atop empty stories. And then too, less towering, the over 40,000 abandoned homes. Whole neighborhoods decaying or razed. Churches, cathedrals, hospitals, schools. Each one a carcinogen in the urban tumor, which slowly metastasized its vacancy, anger and despair up I-75, spreading into Pontiac, Flint, and Saginaw, each with its own rot and exodus, its own stories gone empty.

Robby Cooper turns away from the window. The plane continues its descent into the city's airport.

Beyond the cracked parking lot and cyclone fencing, and down the slope rippling with big bluestem and switchgrass, the Walter P. Reuther Freeway drones with four lanes of westward five o'clock traffic escaping Detroit. An older model Mustang merges onto the interstate from the Orchard Lake Road onramp. Giving it gas, its driver veers in front of other cars, threading a path through the tight configuration. Whole lanes slow with the chain effect of sudden braking. Other drivers signal to switch lanes. They are honked at unforgivingly. The flow backs up to a lurching crawl. The freeway flashes red with the dominoing of taillights.

Robby stands outside an apartment door and watches the Mustang racing unapologetically toward I-696's merger with I-96. The overcast sky threatens rain. Looking at the marbled cloud cover stretched gray to the horizon, Robby scratches feverishly at his upper arm. A raggedy-looking robin lands on top of the cyclone fence. Just as suddenly, it flies away. Robby's green eyes follow it until it's out of sight. He then looks down at the address on the scrap of paper trembling in his hand. The Mustang's waning dual exhaust thunders faintly in the western distance. Robby checks that the number on the paper matches the number on the apartment door. He checks it again. Finger-combing his bangs away from his face, he tucks the longer strands of brown behind his ear. A swatch of hair near his temple is prematurely gray. He inhales a long breath through his nose and looks up into the rusted underside of the second floor walkway. Drying his palms against his jeans, he looks behind him and then looks to the door again. The growl of the Mustang is gone. The freeway is an angry red of brake lights. Exhaling a sigh between his teeth, Robby knocks.

A woman Robby's age opens the door. Her face blanches at the sight of him.

He looks down and his hair falls across his face. He sweeps it aside again. His smile is tight-lipped. "Hi, Tif," he says softly, glancing at her rounded abdomen.

She looks at him as though he is an apparition that might disappear, that hopefully will. She wears a long, blue maternity dress. Her auburn hair is pulled back from her slender face in a ponytail. Her eyes are almond brown. "You shouldn't have come here," she says. "You should have called." Her hand goes to the door, moving as though to close it. "Who gave you the address, anyway?"

"Your mom." He shrugs, looking down at her sandals and the red polish flaking from her toenails. "She said it was good that I come see you face to face."

Tiffany exhales a scornful little laugh through her nose and shakes her head. "She was wrong."

Stuffing his hands into his pockets, he hunches his shoulders towards his ears. He looks at her. "I just wanted to talk."

"I really don't think we have anything to talk about." She crosses her arms between her belly and breasts. "I don't expect anything from you if that's what you're worried about."

"I'm not worried..." He shrugs again. "I just thought that we could talk."

Rain begins to fall, dinging off the hoods of the cars behind him. He looks toward the noise and then back at her.

Tiffany hugs her arms tighter against her body. She glances out at the rain and then back at him. "Is this something you have to do for your program? Are you supposed to talk to people that you might have—"

He shakes his head. "No, I'm not here because—"

"Because I'm not hurt or mad at you, not anymore. That night was a mistake, but it's done. It happened." Her hand goes to her belly and rubs gentle circles. "I really don't expect anything from you or want anything. You've got your own problems. This one's mine...and it's not even a problem, okay? I'm fine."

Robby looks over his shoulder at the water suddenly sheeting down over the cars and asphalt. He looks back at her. "We can't even just talk...just for a minute?" he says, raising his voice above the racket of the downpour.

She studies his face. "You're tan."

He nods. "I guess."

"That place was in Florida, wasn't it?"

"Yeah."

"It was a cold winter here." She shakes her head. "Almost seems like you were being rewarded."

"It wasn't a picnic."

She says nothing. The left side of her mouth nicks up into a disbelieving, mean smile.

He shivers. "Can we, though? Can we just talk?"

"Aren't we talking now?"

"Tif."

She combs her fingers into her hair, squeezing her palms against the side of her head. "What, then? What do you want to say?"

The water slashes in at an angle, soaking his hoodie. He looks at her and his bangs fall across his face again. He shrugs his hands at her. "Do you think I could come in?"

The static hish of the rain soundtracks a frozen moment between them.

Tiffany sighs and then steps back, opening the door wider. "I don't have much time. I need to get ready. I'm covering for someone at work this afternoon." When he doesn't move, she motions with her hand, gesturing him inside with her fingers in a movement that might be used to swat away a mosquito. "Come on. Just don't plan to stay long."

The apartment's kitchen, living room, and dining area are all in the same small space. The chair, coffee table, and sofa look worn and ready for replacement. There's no dining room table. Tiffany walks past Robby and sits in the recliner. Her hands go to her belly and rub, as though trying to predict a future from a crystal ball.

"I just moved in last month," she says. "I'm just starting to put the place together." She smooths her hand over the frayed arm of the chair. "This is the furniture that came with the place."

Standing on the mat near the door, Robby looks around. "It's nice," he says.

"No it isn't."

He nods, pushing his hands into the pockets of his hoodie. A moment passes and then, "Are you still at the dealership?"

She looks at him for a few seconds. "You can sit down."

He smiles and his lips buckle in against his teeth. "Okay. Thanks." He unzips his hoodie, takes it off, and holds it in his hand. He bends toward his laces.

"You don't have to take off your shoes. You're not going to hurt this carpet."

He walks over to the couch and sits, draping the soaked hoodie across his legs. "Are you still at Shuette's?" he asks. He watches the motion of her circling hands.

She nods. "Still at the reception desk, but not for much longer. Dan said that he'll start training me for a title clerk position after the baby is born."

Robby flips his hair away with a snap of his head. He nods thoughtfully. "That a good deal?"

"Better than what I have. It's high stress, but a lot better pay."

He glances up at the sound of footsteps coming from the upstairs apartment. Then he looks at her again. "That's cool, right? I mean, good for you and everything…the better pay."

She shrugs slightly. "What about you? Are you working?"

He shakes his head. Running his fingernails up his arm, he leaves four white tracks in his tanned skin. "I just got back yesterday." He brushes at the tracks. "I'm going to talk to Ty, but not about working." He takes a breath and then releases it. "I don't think he'd give me my job back."

"I wouldn't think so," she says, smirking.

"I need to talk to him though." He looks at the floor. "To apologize."

The muffled sound of the downpour outside fills the room. Tiffany pushes her palms against the arms of the chair and raises the leg rest. Immediately after, her hands go back to the business of rubbing circling calm into her womb.

Robby looks up and watches. "Does it kick?"

She glances at him and the tight purse of her lips suggests that the question is none of his business. "Not exactly. He moves, though. I can feel him moving."

His face brightens. He smiles. "Him? It's a boy?"

"What did you want to talk about, Robby?"

A muted chime vibrates from his pants pocket. He takes out his cell phone and looks at the screen. It reads *Mom*. He presses a button, sending it to voicemail. He looks at Tiffany and stuffs the phone back into his pocket. "I don't know, Tif...everything, I guess."

She smiles coldly. "Is there an everything, Robby?"

He scoots forward on the cushion, rubbing his palms over his knees. "I think so. Don't you think so?" He blinks.

She looks into his eyes, her head shaking slowly, certainly, from side to side. "No. I don't. I really don't."

"It's mine, though, right? I'd heard, and then your mom said—"

She pulls up on the lever and slams the leg rest back into the recliner. "Yes, it's yours. It's yours because you showed up to a party high and started telling me how much you loved me. You found me down in the basement drunk, and you lied to me, and then you fucked me." Tears well in her eyes and she brushes them away with her fingertips. "I didn't hear anything from you after, and when I finally heard something, I heard that you were out of state in rehab. You didn't even—" She takes a deep breath and exhales it slowly.

Robby watches his finger and thumb pick at a loose thread on the couch. "That's not fair. You weren't drunk," he mutters.

"What did you—"

"I didn't lie to you." He looks up at her and into her eyes. "I've had feelings for you since high school. I always—"

She crosses her arms. "Shut up, Robby. Just shut up, okay? I don't want to hear about any of this. I wish you wouldn't have even come here." Taking a breath, she catches her cracking voice. "Why'd you come here?"

He glances toward the window at the water coming down the glass in wormy lines. He lets go of the thread and squeezes his forearm in his hand. "You talk about things when you're in, things you want to make right. That's what they want you to talk about. My mom told me about you...about the—" He looks at her. "I would have called, you know. I was only allowed to talk to one person, though. That was part of the program. I got to talk to my mom once every two weeks. That's it."

Tiffany looks at him, almost through him. "I don't want to hear—"

"For the last three months, you were who I talked about. In group, in one-on-one. I talked about you...you and the baby. I just want to do something right. I want to play some kind of part—"

"No."

He looks at her, eyes wide. Outside, the rain is an indecipherable whisper.

She shakes her head. "We're not part of your recovery. We're not going to be the thing that makes you feel better about yourself, okay? You're just going to have to—"

"I don't mean it that way," he says. He bows and holds his head between his hands. "It's not about my recovery or... I just want to help. I want to be involved in some way."

"That's fine, but I'm saying no. I don't need any help from my mom, and I don't need any help from you...especially not you."

The heating unit kicks on and drones into the room.

He closes his eyes and squeezes his forehead in his hand. "Why? I don't understand. I just want to do something..." A tear breaks from his eye and he smears it across his cheek. "I mean, he's my son, too. Like it or not—"

"I want you to leave."

He looks at her. "Tif—"

"I know what you're thinking." Using the arms of the chair, she pushes herself slowly to standing. "A boy should have his father in his life." She looks toward the window. "That's probably true most of the time. But you're an addict and a liar and a thief. I don't want that in my life or his life." She turns back toward him. "I just want you to stay the hell away from me, okay?" She glowers at him with stony eyes. "I should have never let you come in here."

Dropping his face into his hands, he releases a choked sob. His body shakes. Then, he stops himself, breathing in a strained breath through his teeth and exhaling it into his palms. "Jesus Christ, Tif," he whispers. "You won't let me be any part of this? You're really saying that you won't let—"

"Robby, just go. That's what I'm saying. Just go." She walks to the door and opens it. She looks at the floor. The sound of the rain is like colossal radio static.

Pulling his hoodie over his head, he looks out at the cold, wet world waiting for him.

~*~

Outside her apartment, he turns back to her framed in the doorway. "Could you call me, at least? Or, call my mom? Would you at least do that?"

Her eyebrows knit together. "Call you? What are you—"

"When he's born." His voice cracks. "Could you just call me when he's born?"

To the south, the freeway is a misty river of brake lights.

She looks down at the well-worn welcome mat. Her hand rubs her belly. "I don't know," she says, pushing the door toward him. Her hand stops rubbing. "I don't think so." She closes the door.

Tears stream down his face. "You weren't drunk!" he shouts above the noise of the falling water. He turns, flips up his hood, and runs through the rain toward his car.

~*~

Sitting in the driver's seat with the engine running, Robby turns on the radio. Bruce Springsteen sings something about time drifting away and leaving you with nothing but boring memories from better days. He turns the radio off.

He squeezes the wheel in both hands and chews his lower lip. He shakes his head. After a moment of staring through the windshield, he fishes the cell phone out of his pocket and listens to his voicemail:

"Robby, it's Mom. Grandpa Otto wants you to stop out to his place when you get a chance. He just called. I tried to give him your number, but he said that he wants to see you in person. Soon as you can, okay? Don't keep him waiting too long. You know how he gets. Call me, too. I want to know how things went with Tiffany. Okay? Okay. Well, bye. I'll talk to you soon. I love you, and I'm so proud of you. You're doing great. Everything just keeps getting better from here, okay? You just need to—"

He tosses the phone onto the passenger seat. It bounces once and lands down in the passenger seat footwell. His mother's voice keeps talking faintly.

He flips it the middle finger.

Shivering and wet, he turns on the heater. The vents blow cold air over him.

Outside, the world undulates through the rain-wrecked windshield. Reaching to shift into *drive*, he slumps forward and buries his face in his arms against the steering wheel.

Robby stands in the middle of a street in Fox Ridge Meadows. He pushes his hair from his face. In the distance, a lawnmower buzzes. Sunlight coming out of the east glares off the windshields of the trucks parked at the curb in front of him. Shielding his eyes, he takes a step forward, but then stops. The six adjoined townhouses beyond the trucks are identical, painted an olive green that is faded and peeling in places. The three trucks parked near the curb each bear the Busy Bee Painting logo, which is a smiling cartoon honey bee flying with a paint brush in its foreleg and a can of green paint where it would otherwise be carrying pollen. The same paint drips from its stinger. Just beneath the picture reads the company motto: "Oh honey, we'll treat you right!"

Robby takes a deep breath and then exhales a long sigh.

A prep crew of guys works on one of the units. Some use power drills to remove downspouts or shutters. Others tape sheets of plastic over windows. Another crew uses power washers to knock loose paint from the units that have already been prepped. The guys shout back and forth to each other above the noise of the tools. Robby watches them. He swipes the sweat from his forehead with his palm.

A red-headed man in t-shirt and jeans walks across the front lawns surveying the work. "You guys are going too slow," he shouts. "These guys are going to be spraying water right up your asses if you don't pick up the pace." He points at a young guy up on an extension ladder removing a faux shutter. "Although you'd probably like that, wouldn't you, Eric?"

Eric reaches into his front pocket as though looking for something and then pulls out his middle finger.

The red-headed man laughs. "All right, all right, just give me a little more hustle, will ya?"

A driver taps his horn. Robby jumps and then steps closer to the trucks so the car can get past him. He waves apologetically to the driver.

When Robby focuses again on the townhouses, the red-headed man is walking toward him. His paint-splattered t-shirt has the same bee on it that's on the trucks. His laughing smile is gone and he shakes his head disbelievingly.

"That you, Robby?"

Robby swallows. He nods and waves. "Hey, Ty."

Ty stops a few feet from him and crosses his freckled arms. A ghost of sun block haunts his nose and forehead. "Holy shit." He shakes his head disgustedly. "I heard you were back."

Robby crosses his own arms over his chest and shrugs his shoulders. "Been back for a few days." He looks past Ty at the guys working on the houses. "I don't recognize anyone."

Ty looks back at his men. "Pretty much a whole new crew. Always lots of turnover season to season. Nature of the business." He points. "That's Steve working the power washer. He was on prep with you last fall." He turns and faces Robby again. "Terry Jones is over on another unit doing trim. Remember him?"

Robby looks at the ground and nods.

"Moved him up, too. Making painting wages now." Ty watches his own fingers scratch his upper arm. "Suppose I would have moved you up too if things had been different."

Robby sniffs in a breath and looks up into the tops of the tall evergreens planted throughout the complex.

"I wouldn't go out of your way to say hi to Terry," Ty says.

Robby shrugs. "I never did really know him that well."

"Yeah." Ty leans against the tailgate of one of his trucks and fishes a pack of cigarettes from his pocket. "You look like you put on a little weight." He shakes a smoke up from the pack and pulls it out with his lips. "Wasn't much to you when you were working for me," he says, talking around the cigarette. "Regular stick man."

"They got it so food tasted good to me again. They had good cooks."

Ty pulls a lighter from his pants pocket and touches a flame to the end of the cigarette. He takes a drag, exhales, and then looks into Robby's face. The side of his mouth nicks up into an unwelcoming smile. "So, what are you doing here? Casing the place?"

Robby winces. "I just thought I'd stop by. I was on my way to my grandpa's. I called the office, and Shelly said you guys were here."

Ty takes another drag and then studies the cigarette between his fingers. "Your grandpa still in the same house?"

He nods. "Yeah."

"Going from your ma's place in Livonia down to Lincoln Park by way of Southfield sounds like a pretty fucked-up shortcut to me."

Robby shifts his weight to his other foot. He crosses his arms and stuffs his fingers into his armpits. He shrugs. "I wanted to talk to you, I guess."

"You guess?" Ty exhales smoke into the air above them. He rubs his hand over his face. "Why? You looking for work?"

Robby scratches the back of his head. "I'd take it if you're offering."

Ty shakes his head and sniffs a laugh out his nostrils. "Jesus, but you got balls."

He pumps his palms toward him. "That's not why I came. I'm just saying that I'd take a job if you have one...if you need someone."

"I don't." He points at Robby's chest. "And if I did, I sure as fuck wouldn't hire your sorry ass." He drops his barely-smoked cigarette and steps on it. "You're just goddamn lucky I've had six months to cool down."

Robby nods. "I know. I—"

"I had five bids come through in the last couple weeks. It's got me in a good mood. Otherwise, I'd probably be picking your teeth out of my knuckles right now." He crosses his arms again.

Robby's face pales. He swallows. "Jesus, Ty."

"Come on. Come on. I got work to do. What the fuck are you here for, Robby? Just looking at you is bringing all that shit back up." He fingers out his pack again.

Robby stuffs his hands into his pockets and shrugs. "I want to make amends," he says.

Ty smirks. "What is that, rehab talk?"

Robby shrugs again. "It's just what I want to do."

"How you plan to do that?" He lights his cigarette.

"I thought I'd come back at the end of the day and clean all the sprayers for you." He looks at him. "Tomorrow, too, if you want."

Ty exhales and then laughs. "And that would make us even in your book, huh?"

Robby rubs his palm against his forehead. "The trucks, too. I can wash all the trucks for you."

Taking a drag, he stares at Robby. He blows the smoke into his face. "You stole my equipment. You took all the sprayers, all the power washers, and all but one of the extension ladders." He holds up a finger as he lists each item. "You left me with nothing, and you're telling me that you're going to clean some sprayers and wash my fucking trucks?"

A few of the guys stop working and look toward their boss' raised voice. All of the power washers have been turned off.

Robby takes his hands from his pockets and shrugs his palms into the air. "Well, just…Ty. I mean, just tell me—"

He flicks his cigarette into Robby's chest. "Get the fuck outta here."

Robby brushes at the sparks. "Ty—"

Ty comes off the truck and shoves him back a step. "I mean it, you little prick. Get out of here before I tear you a new asshole."

He stands stunned. He blinks. "I'm trying to apologize here. I'm trying to make—"

Ty grabs the front of Robby's hoodie in both hands and launches him into the street.

He runs slap-footed with the throw and windmills his arms to keep himself from falling. He turns back toward Ty. He stands in the middle of the street. "You got it all back," he shouts. "The cops nailed me before I even had the chance to try to sell it. You got all your shit back, man."

Ty takes a step toward him. "Are you doing this? Are you fucking standing there and arguing with me?"

Robby takes a few paces backwards. "Well you did. You got it back."

A car comes and forces him backpedaling to the other side of the street.

Ty marches across the asphalt at him. "Did I, Robby? Did I get my fucking shit back?"

He stares, rubbing his hand over his head. "Didn't you?"

Ty spits on the ground. "Yeah, sure I did…about five weeks later, asshole."

Rubbing his fingers on his forehead, Robby furrows his brow. "Five weeks?"

Ty looks behind him where three of his guys are standing by the trucks looking ready to cross the street. He gestures them away with a swat of his arm. "Get back to work. There's nothing going on here." He watches until they retreat. Then he turns back toward Robby, his neck red up to his ears.

"I don't get... Five weeks?" Robby pushes his fingers through his hair. "Why five weeks?"

Ty takes a step forward driving Robby a few paces onto the lawn. "Evidence, fuck-face. They held it all as evidence. I almost lost my whole fucking business because of you."

"But the lawyer had pictures. That's what he showed...he had pictures."

He points a finger in Robby's face. "I was in the middle of two jobs. I had bids in on three others. You know how much that fucking cost me? I had to let guys go...guys with families. I had to borrow money from my old man just to cover my loans. Half that shit I didn't even own yet." He plants his hands into Robby's chest and shoves him to the ground. "I almost had to shit can the whole fucking thing."

Robby tucks his legs up into his stomach and covers his head with his arms. "I'm sorry, man. I didn't know. I didn't. I was all fucked up."

Ty looms over him. "What I should do is call Terry Jones over here. He didn't get Unemployment. Had to move back in with his folks." He looks back over his shoulder toward the distance. "I should call him over here so he can tell you about it." He glares back at him. "Maybe you can do his laundry for him or wash his car."

Robby's hair hangs in his face. "I'm sorry, Ty. I really am. At the time...at the time, it seemed like the only way." He sniffs in a breath and clears his throat. "I was really in a bad place. Like I was cornered—"

Ty hisses a laugh between his teeth. "So then you fuck me over."

Robby inches a pace away on his elbow. He flips his bangs from his eyes. "It wasn't about... I mean, I wasn't thinking like that. I was desperate. I wasn't thinking about what it would do to you. It just didn't feel like there was any other way out. I wasn't thinking straight, man."

Ty looks to his right. Robby follows his gaze. At the next house, a man stands in his yard staring at them. He holds a small stack of mail.

"Fuck," Ty whispers. He reaches his hand down to Robby. "Get up."

Robby takes his hand, and Ty yanks him to his feet. They look back at the man who lingers before going up his stoop and into his house. Ty shakes his head. "Look at that. You're still fucking making trouble for me."

Robby slaps at the dirt and grass stains on his pants. "I'm not trying to make trouble. I just want to try to make things right. I know an apology is nothing. It doesn't do anything. I want.... I mean, I'll work for you for free. Just tell me something that would even start—"

"Fuck off, Robby. That's what you can do."

Robby takes a step forward. "Ty—"

Ty shoves him away. "I said to fuck off."

He looks at Ty's right hand squeezed into a fist. He closes his eyes and sticks his chin out. "Deck me, then. Knock out a few of my teeth. Break my nose. Whatever you want. I deserve it."

Ty looks at his fist and then unclenches it. Shaking his head, he turns and starts to walk away. "Stay away from the 40-bar, Robby."

He opens his eyes. "Ty? Ty, just hold on—"

"And if you come around me again, I'll file a restraining order."

~*~

Ty crosses the street shaking his head. His guys shoot looks Robby's way while they work in slow motion.

A screwdriver unhurriedly backs a screw from a shutter. A hand smooths and then resmooths the tape that holds plastic over a window.

Ty scans his crew. "What is this," he shouts, "a break? Get back at it, goddamnit!"

One of the guys up on a ladder looks over at Robby. "Who's the douche bag, boss?"

Ty glances back at Robby one last time. "Nobody." He turns back to his crew. "Don't worry about it. Just get your asses back to work."

~*~

Jogging to his car, Robby brushes away the tears welling in his eyes. "Fuck."

A washer fires up behind him and hammers away at the side of a house.

"You okay? Did he hurt you?"

Robby stops.

The man who was watching them earlier sits on his stoop going through envelopes. Robby looks at the cell phone in the man's hand. Quiet for a moment, he rubs his fingers over his forehead thoughtfully. "Yeah, I'm fine. Nothing I didn't deserve, anyway." He snorts in a breath. "He's got strict rules about respecting the customer's property. I crossed the line, and he let me know it. That's all."

The man looks over at Ty's trucks.

~*~

Robby slips into his car, starts it up, and pulls away from the curb. He pushes his wrist under his misted eyes. Looking up a moment later, he grabs the wheel and snaps his car back into his lane.

The driver in the other lane lays on his horn and glares at him as he goes by.

"Fuck you," Robby shouts.

~*~

Robby drives on the Southfield Freeway. He pulls down his visor, blocking the sunlight glaring off the back windows of the cars in front of him. Listening to WRIF out of Detroit, he hammers his thumbs on the steering wheel to the beat of Led Zeppelin's "Black Dog."

He glances at the clock on the dashboard and then pushes the car up to eighty miles an hour.

His phone rings. He pulls it out of his pocket, checks the

screen, and rolls his eyes. He turns down the radio and takes the call. "Hey, Mom. I'm almost there."

"Your grandfather has called me three times already. Where have you been? You left the house an hour and a half ago."

He draws in a breath and sighs. "I went to see somebody."

Jimmy Page's solo whispers from the speakers backed by a haunting of drums.

"Who?" Her voice cracks on the o.

"Just somebody, okay?" He glances at the grass stain on his knee and then back to the highway.

Zeppelin fades out. Robby's mother cries softly on her end.

"Sonuvabitch," he mouths.

~*~

The Rouge River passing under the highway looks like a long mud puddle, choked into a channel with concrete banks. Robby's hand squeezes the steering wheel. "I'm not using, okay? Stop crying. I'm still clean. I just had to go see Ty… You can't think that every time—"

"I don't know what I'm supposed to think," she shouts. She breathes in a staccato breath. "You spend all that time in your room. You don't tell me anything. You sneak out—"

"Calm down. I didn't sneak. Okay? I didn't. I just left. You knew where I was going. I told you I was going to Grandpa's—"

"But then you didn't, did you?"

He switches the phone to his other ear and switches hands on the wheel. "I'm on my way there right now. You can't worry so much, Mom. You can't."

She's quiet a moment. "It feels like that's all I can do."

He exhales. "I gotta go. I'm getting really close to—"

"What did Ty say?"

101.1 glows dimly green from the radio display.

Robby clears his throat. "Not much."

"What, though? He said something."

A semi begins to pass him on his left, a looming shadow. He tightens his grip on the wheel. "He told me to fuck off."

"Robby!"

"What?" He laughs. "You wanted to know."

Quiet a moment, she breathes through her nose and sighs the breath out from her mouth. "Honey, I'm sorry. I shouldn't have raised my voice like I did."

"Mom—"

"I think it's great that you're making an effort to talk to people. Tiffany and Ty weren't very receptive, but you at least tried. That's all you can do." Her voice is cadenced and comforting.

A grey semi-trailer streaked with rust rattles and bangs outside his window. Brown and pink cow snouts press moist at the vents. A mournful, long-lashed eye stares at him. Robby looks away back to the road.

"I'm so proud of you. What you're doing…what you're trying to do. It isn't easy. But it's going to get better every day. It may not feel like it all the—"

"Mom!"

Silence.

He scratches the phone at the side of his head and then puts it back to his ear. "Please stop reading those brochures. Please. You've been saying the same shit to me since I got back."

She sniffs in a hurt breath. "I'm just trying to help."

He holds the phone away from his ear, squeezes it, and then returns it. "I know you're trying to help. You have helped. You gave me a place to stay. You're trusting me with your car. All of that helps. It really does. But no more motivational shit, okay? No more talk about each day getting a little bit better. All of that…it makes me feel like I'm retarded, like I'm six years old or something."

"Okay," she says. "I'll try not to anymore. But I need to know what you need from me. Tell me that at least. None of this is easy for me, either. I'm just as lost—"

"Just give me a little breathing space. Don't stare at me like I'm going to relapse any time I leave the room. Just trust me a little bit. Don't think that you always have to be doing something or saying something to support me."

A motorcycle whines past on his right going at least ninety miles an hour. The rider threads the bike between cars, leaning his body to the left or right, making it look easy. Robby watches his zigzag disappearance.

"Okay," she says, "I can do that. But then I need you to do something for me, too." She pauses. "I need you to tell me how you're doing sometimes. I need you to let me know what you're feeling or thinking. Don't keep me guessing so much. I'm not talking all the time, but just sometimes, so I don't feel in the dark so much."

He watches the last traces of the motorcyclist.

"Robby?"

He nods. "Yeah, okay, I can try to be better about that."

The highway flashes from shadow to light to shadow as he passes under overpasses. The semi full of cows starts up an onramp toward eastbound I-94. The Southfield Freeway becomes Southfield Road. Small Allen Park homes line the side of the highway.

"Good," she says. "That will help." She pauses a moment. "So...what are you thinking or feeling?"

"Are you kidding?"

"Just humor me, okay? Just this time."

He takes a deep breath and puffs his cheeks as he exhales. "I think I'm doing all right. It's been a shitty week, but I'm hanging in there."

She clears her throat and sniffs a breath. "And...and no cravings?"

"Nothing I couldn't handle."

A moment passes.

"Honey, you are doing so—"

"Mom."

"Okay." She laughs. "Okay, I'm sorry. I won't... I'm just glad to hear that you're doing okay."

He forces a smile. "So far so good. One day at a time, right? Each new day is a step forward. Breathe in, breathe out. I got to remember that today is the tomorrow that I worried about yesterday. My clean life is closer than I—"

She laughs. "Okay, Mr. Smarty Pants. Just get to your grandpa's before he calls me again. You know how he can get."

He nods. "Almost there. I'll talk to you soon."

"Okay, bye honey. I love you so—"

"Bye, Mom." He hangs up the phone and sets it on the dashboard. A house with boarded up windows flashes by. Reaching under the driver's seat, Robby pulls out an orange pill bottle. He holds it between his finger and thumb, balancing it on top of the steering wheel.

It gives off a jack-o'-lantern glow in the sunlight.

When he shakes it a few times, it makes the sound of a nearly empty maraca.

Arching his hips up from the seat, he stuffs the bottle deep into his front pocket. He flips his bangs from his face.

AC/DC's "Highway to Hell" plays faintly. He turns it up and plucks the steering wheel with the first two fingers of his right hand.

He passes under the shadow of I-75's overpass and out into the blinding sunlight on the other side.

~*~

The small houses on Mayflower Avenue are packed tightly together with a driveway of space in between each. Bushes against the fronts of the homes are carefully trimmed, and the little lawns are well-tended. Most of the awning-covered stoops have pots of flowers and wicker chairs. Strolling along the sidewalk, a gray-haired couple waves to Robby as he drives past.

He waves back. A moment later he pulls his car over to the curb.

His grandfather's house is a brick ranch with an enclosed porch. The small front lawn looks as neatly maintained as a golf course fairway. The lamppost near the end of the driveway is on, glowing dimly in the sunlight. With its crown spread as wide as the roof, a sugar maple towers behind the house. Its bare branches show only a stubble of green spring bloom.

He sits in his car staring at the tree. His hand clenches and unclenches the wheel.

~*~

Robby comes out of his daze when the door to the porch opens and his Grandpa Otto shuffles out onto the stoop. A tall man, he is lean with a thick head of white hair. His brow is rutted with waves of wrinkles, and deep lines run from either nostril down to his jaw, framing his mouth. He wears a checkered shirt and pressed khakis cinched tight around his thin waist with a belt.

He points and his mouth moves.

Robby rolls down his window. "What?"

"What the hell you doing sitting in the car, boy? Your legs broken?"

Robby gets out. He talks while jogging across the street. "Just looking at your tree."

"What?"

"Your tree in the backyard."

"What about it?"

He stops a few feet from the lowest step of the stoop. Looking up at the topmost branches peaking over the house, he points. "I remember climbing it when I was a kid. I'd really get up there."

"You're still a kid," his grandfather says, looking him up and down. He shakes his head. "They didn't allow scissors in that place or what?"

"What?"

Otto crosses his arms. "Your hair wants cutting, boy…something fierce."

Robby flips his bangs from his eyes. He exhales. "How you doing, Grandpa?"

He looks at him, smiles, and then hobbles stiff-legged down the steps. "Come on, let me show you something." He pushes past.

"What do you want to show me?"

Otto keeps walking. "Just come on."

Shaking his head, Robby watches the old man's determined, staggering gait. He smiles and then follows.

~*~

They go up the driveway, through a gate in the chain-link fence, and into the backyard.

Otto points to a plot of dirt out of which grow tiny green plants. "Cherry tomatoes," he says.

Robby looks at them. "Nice."

Otto stands over the plants surveying them with his hands on his hips. He runs knobby fingers through his shock of hair. "Dug this all up myself." He crosses his arms. "Your grandmother loved cherry tomatoes. Ate 'em like candy." He rubs a hand back and forth over his head. "She always wanted me to plant some, and here I am planting them now. That would have made her chuckle." He laughs disbelievingly in his throat. "I don't even like 'em."

Robby scratches his forehead. "Well, my mom likes them. You can give them to her."

Otto makes a disgruntled noise and then turns and faces the sugar maple. He puts his hands on his hips. "Well, there's your tree, boy. You gonna climb it?"

He looks up into the height of it. "I'd probably break my neck now."

Shielding their eyes from the sun, they both study the upmost branches.

"Probably so," Otto says. He crosses his arms and looks around his yard. "Hey, why don't you help me get the picnic table out here?"

Robby shrugs. "Sure."

~*~

In the back corner of the yard an aluminum storage shed is painted red with white trim to resemble a barn. Otto pulls a set of keys from his pocket and flips through them.

Robby winces, watching his swollen fingers struggle to undo the padlock. "You want me to do it?"

Otto looks over his shoulder at him and then back to the lock. "I'm fine. Not quite an invalid yet." He turns the key again and the lock gives. He removes it from the staple and flips aside the hasp.

Opening the doors, he reveals the picnic table at the back of the shed buried under yard tools and other lawn furniture.

Otto starts pointing. "Move that stuff out of there so we can get at the table."

Robby sighs and grabs the handles of the wheelbarrow, backing it up out of the shed and onto the lawn. "You having people over?"

"Nah. I just like to eat outside when the weather is nicer." He takes a shovel from the shed and leans its handle into the lilac bushes.

Robby wheels out the grill next to the wheelbarrow.

"Put that up on the patio."

"What?"

"The grill. Put it up on the patio for me."

Rolling his eyes, he drags the grill jostling across the yard. Its lid slides off onto the ground. He looks at his grandfather, standing with his hands on his hips. His head bobs around on his neck, surveying the inside of the shed.

"Careful with that, boy," he says without turning to look.

Robby fits the lid back onto the grill and drags it the rest of the way to the patio. He starts back toward Otto. "I checked it. It looks okay. Good thing, too. Those steel lids can be pretty fragile."

"If you're done being a smartass, you might as well put the birdbath out, too," Otto says.

Robby stops and crosses his arms. "This is going to be all fucking day," he mutters.

Otto looks back at him. "Little hustle, boy. I don't want to be all day at this."

Robby jogs over to the shed and crouches down to the cement base of the birdbath.

"Lift with your legs."

"I know." He hefts it up, adjusts his grip, and grunts it over to the other corner of the yard.

"Not back there. Put it up closer to the house. I won't be able to see the birds if it's way back there."

He lugs it along the length of the yard's perimeter.

"Good. Right there. Not too close to the fence or you won't be able to get the basin on it."

Laughing, Robby stands and stretches his back. "I wouldn't have come if I knew you were going to put me to work."

Otto makes a disappointed sounding noise with his lips. "You sound like your Uncle Jack when he was your age."

"What?"

"Nothing. Just get the basin. And be careful. It doesn't look it, but it's heavier than the bottom."

Breathing heavily, Robby walks over and bends.

"Legs."

"Yeah, yeah."

He staggers the weight across the yard and fits the basin on top of the pedestal. Sweat drips down his forehead. When he turns back, his grandfather has a hoop of garden hose over his shoulder.

"I'll hook this up and fill the bath. Put the Adirondack chairs over near the grill."

Walking back to the shed, Robby pounds the bottom of a fist against the top of the other. Shaking his head, he cradles one of the chairs in his arms and hauls it to the patio.

Otto crouches at the faucet and twists the hose's nozzle onto it. He stops a moment and looks over at Robby. "Your mom says you're doing pretty good."

He sets the chair down and mops his sleeve across his forehead. He takes a deep breath through his nose and exhales it. "I guess."

"You working?"

"Not yet, but I have quite a few applications out."

Otto nods. "Good. Keeping busy will help keep your mind off things. Idle hands and all that."

Robby crosses his arms. "That's what my counselor said."

Otto looks at him over his shoulder. "Right now, it's what I'm saying. Keeping busy is the best thing." He holds his gaze on him before turning the spigot. The hose begins to writhe and then a moment later the nozzle shoots off. Water pools on the ground. "Piece of garbage!" he shouts, turning the water off again. He stands up, and the knee of his pant leg is soaked. He brushes at it. "Goddamn it anyway."

"You want me to do it?"

Otto waves him off and starts toward the house. "I got it. Just get the other chair."

Robby returns with the other chair and sets it close to the first. Grimacing, he picks at a sliver lodged in his palm.

Returning from inside, Otto kneels at the faucet with a crescent wrench and twists the hose coupling until it's tight. When he turns the faucet, water pours out the other end. "Fill that bath, will ya?" he says, slipping the wrench into his back pocket. He uses the windowsill to pull himself up to his feet.

Robby drags the streaming hose over to the birdbath. He puffs his cheeks and exhales a slow sigh. "You thinking of getting involved in Detroit's human slave trafficking, Grandpa? Am I your first?"

Otto clears his throat, producing a sound like a laugh. "Is smart-mouthing supposed to be part of your recovery?"

Watching the water swirl into the basin, Robby smiles.

Otto takes a few steps and stands only feet behind him. "Your dad used to help me do all this. All of it. Fall too. Raking leaves and putting everything away. He was a good son."

Robby nods slowly. His left eye twitches.

"Course, the other boys..."

He holds the hose absently, staring into the yard next door. A robin hops along the ground in one of the bare patches of dirt in the neighbor's lawn. It stops a few times and stares intently near its feet, looking ready to pluck a worm. Then, without any warning or indication, it flies away. Robby wipes the back of his hand over his eyes. He gazes up into an empty blue sky.

The water stops. He looks at the hose and then back at his grandfather crouched at the spigot.

Water spills from the edges of the overfull basin.

Otto smiles. "I think it's full, boy. Gotta keep your mind on what you're doing." He stands again. "Let's get that picnic table out here."

The hose drops from Robby's hand.

"Hey, quit half-assing. Wind that up and put it near the house."

Robby gathers the hose in loops around his shoulder and tosses the coil of it near the spigot. Then, he meets his grandfather at the shed. Climbing over the picnic table, he gets on the far side of it and hefts his end. Otto lifts his side and, when they get it out onto the lawn, he sets it down again.

"Slow down, boy." He takes a deep breath and looks across the table. "Want some advice? Don't get old. It's all about watching yourself slowly fall apart."

Robby waits, picking a fingernail against the tip of the sliver. He grimaces. "Why do you keep the picnic table in the shed, anyway?"

Otto opens and closes his enflamed fingers. "What?"

"Why not just leave it on the patio? Then you wouldn't have to do this."

Otto rubs his palms against each other. A nostril arches in a sneer. "Because it's wood, Einstein. Leave it out winter after winter and it warps. Get water melting on it, freezing, melting again. Eventually it rots." He points at Robby. "You gotta take care of things." He massages the palm of his right hand between the forefinger and thumb of the left. "Otherwise things turn to shit."

Robby looks at the grass and shrugs. He spits. A dog barks from somewhere in the neighborhood. Another dog answers it and then another.

"Come on, pick up your end."

They set the table down one more time before finally getting it up onto the patio. Otto rolls and stretches his back, moaning his aches.

Robby looks back at the shed. "Did we get everything?"

Looking, Otto furrows his brow a moment. "This lawn wants fertilizer, but I'll do that myself. You put too much and you'll burn it up." He points at the bench in front of Robby. "Go ahead and sit down. You want something to drink?"

He shakes his head. "Nah, I'm good." He nibbles his lower lip. "I'm probably going to take off, Grandpa."

Otto points at the bench. "You got time to sit down for a minute. What the hell's your hurry?"

Robby sighs. He throws one leg over the bench, straddling it.

Otto sits on the other side, giving a satisfied and exhausted grunt. "Oh boy," he says, looking around. "Nice day."

Robby looks off toward the neighbor's yard, studying the bare patches of dry earth.

"Grubs," Otto says after a moment.

Robby looks at him.

He holds up his hand with his finger and thumb an inch apart. "About that big. June bug grubs. They eat the grass roots. They can wipe out a lawn in a hurry."

Robby nods and then looks back toward the neighbor's lawn.

"They get his lawn every year," Otto says, pointing toward the neighbor's yard. "Every year he puts down new seed and covers it with hay. He waters it religiously." He snorts a laugh and shakes his head. "Never treats for the grubs, though. His lawn looks terrible every spring."

Robby studies the arid patches of earth.

"I don't even think he knows what's happening. He sure as hell never asks me why my lawn looks so good."

Robby turns back. "Why don't you just tell him?"

He swats his hand indifferently toward the neighbor's yard. "Not my business. He can figure things out on his own. Moved in here five years ago but never could find the courtesy to introduce himself."

"Did you introduce yourself?"

Otto looks at him. "Full of piss and vinegar today, aren't you? What, you got an answer for everything all of a sudden?"

They sit for a moment, not speaking. Upper branches of the maple move and groan in a wind that moves nothing on the ground.

Robby runs his fingers through his hair and scans the yard.

~*~

A robin lands at the birdbath. Getting in, it dips its head into the basin and flutters arcs of water over itself.

"Thanks for helping me out today, boy." He pats his palm on top of Robby's hand. "We got a lot done."

He looks at his hand and then at Otto. He shrugs and flips his hair from his eyes. "No problem."

Otto looks at his bangs and smiles. "Got scissors right in the house. Got a bowl that would probably fit your head, too. We can take care of that."

"You're looking a little shaggy yourself."

Otto pats his palms over his head. "You got me there. It's been awhile since I've had the chance to get to the barber." He sets his puffy hands on the table, one over the other. "I'm trying not to do too much driving."

Robby nods, though his eyes look puzzled. He scratches his nose. "Gas prices a little high for you, Grandpa?"

"No," he says, rubbing a hand over the gray stubble on his cheeks. "Not exactly that." He traces a finger slowly along the inside curves of his ear and then looks at the tip. He flicks something away. "Just not supposed to be driving right now...doctor's orders."

"Why, what's wrong?"

Otto waves a hand through the air dismissively. "Nothing. Just a precaution. Just checking out something with my eyes." He looks at Robby. His eyes narrow. "Get that look off your face, will ya? Eyes can go bad. It's that getting older thing I was telling you about. It will happen to you, too. Then you'll understand. Every day brings some new little surprise. I'm like a car right after the warranty expires." He looks off toward the neighbor's barren yard and shakes his head. "Pretty soon I'll be pissing myself every half hour and walking around with a dump in my drawers like a two-year-old."

Robby stifles a laugh. "Jesus, Grandpa."

"What?" He laughs too. "Laugh to keep from crying, right? That's all you can do, boy."

"I guess so."

Otto stretches his arms out in front of him, yawns, and then sets both palms flat on the table. "So, yeah, no driving for me for a little while." He looks at Robby and smiles distantly. "I guess that's one of the reasons why I called you to come over here."

Robby worries the thumb of his right hand between the fingers and thumb of his left. He watches his hands. "You want me to drive you somewhere?"

He nods, scratching one of his bushy eyebrows. "Actually, a few somewheres. It'd be a road trip. About a week, maybe a little more."

Robby looks at him out from under his bangs. "A road trip?"

"Yeah. I want to go to Flint to see your Uncle Jack and then up to Traverse City to see your Uncle Paul." He looks over his shoulder up into the branches of the maple. "It's been too long since I've been to their places."

Robby throws his other leg over the bench and sits facing his grandfather. He leans on his elbows and rests his fingers against his mouth. "A week? Grandpa, I just got—"

"Well, I wouldn't expect you to do it for nothing. I'd pay you. You're not working right now, so it would give you a little spending..."

Robby finger-combs his hair over the top of his head with swift swipes of his splayed hand. He looks at the table top. "It's not about money. You wouldn't have to... It's just that I don't think—"

"It wouldn't be all work, boy. I was thinking that I could bring my fishing gear. I'd take you on the Au Sable where your dad and I used to go. I got another set of waders that I bet would fit you. If not, I'll buy you a pair. You've never been fly fishing, have you? Something like that is good for the soul...helps a guy think things through."

Robby sighs and looks at the ground. He speaks quietly. "Dad was always after me to go fishing with him." He smooths a finger back and forth over the table edge. "He bought me all the gear for one of my birthdays."

Otto smiles. "Well, there you go. You're already all set to—"

"I sold it."

His face falls. "Sold...?" He blinks. "Well, that doesn't matter. Like I said, I'd get you waders. I have three different rods down in the basement. Gear isn't an issue."

Robby shakes his head. "I can't. I got counseling I need to go to yet. Outpatient. It's all part of the rehab." He squeezes both palms over the sides of his head. "Plus I'm waiting on all those applications. If I get a call, I have to be here. I need to get—"

"You got a phone. If someone calls you for an interview, then we come back. We won't be more than four hours away."

He touches his fingers along the outside of his pants pocket. "Grandpa, I can't. I have to be here for the counseling sessions. If it looks like I'm not—"

Otto flips a hand in the air and then swats it at him. "Talk to your counselor. Hell, a road trip with your grandpa? He'd probably think that'd be good for you. Those guys are usually pretty laid back. If you just ask him—"

"I haven't even met him yet. Or her. I don't have any idea what this person is like. It'd look pretty bad if the first call I make is to try to get out of counseling. They already put me down as having attitude problems at the other place. I gotta try to play this—"

Otto waves both hands at him as though closing an invisible lid. "All right. All right. The hell with it. I won't go." He sets his hands on the edge and pushes himself to standing. He talks while sidestepping out between the bench and the table. "I'm going to go in. It's getting too hot out here. I'm going to take a nap, so you'll have to let yourself out."

"Grandpa..."

"Grandpa, nothing. Just let yourself out."

Robby looks down into the table as though wanting to find some answer etched there.

~*~

Holding the screen door, Otto pauses in the doorway to the house. He looks off toward the tomato seedlings. "I just thought it'd be good for us. The little road trip, some fishing. Pretty stupid idea really, now that I think about it."

Robby starts to stand up. "Grand—"

"Thanks again for helping me with the furniture, boy. Probably really can't ask for more than that." He steps into the house and thunks the wooden door shut between them.

Robby drops back onto the bench. Gritting his teeth, he looks up into the high branches of the sugar maple. His hand goes to the outside of his pocket again and squeezes.

~*~

The room's one window is covered by a dark Venetian blind. The sunlight behind it is only a rumor. There's a lamp on the desk and a lamp turned on next to Robby where he sits in a leather chair. He's slumped in his seat with his elbows on the arm rests. His hands hang from his wrists above his pant pockets. He rubs his middle fingers back and forth over his thumbs making muted snaps. His hair hangs in his eyes.

On the other side of the coffee table, the therapist jots something down on the legal pad resting against his crossed legs. He is a shorter, thin man with a head of wavy salt and pepper hair. He wears a sports coat over a Detroit Pistons t-shirt with blue jeans and black monk straps on his feet. His eyes smile.

"And so," he says, looking up at Robby, "you stole the equipment to try to get money for Oxycontin?"

"Yeah."

"Thousands of dollars' worth...for personal use?" He smiles, tilting his head to the side. "Is that correct?"

Robby looks coldly out from under his hair. "That's what I just said."

The therapist scratches his head. "That's quite a bit of Oxy, even at street prices."

He shrugs. "Like I said, I wasn't thinking straight at the time. I wasn't doing any math. I just needed money and the equipment was there."

The therapist nods and then switches his legs. He taps the tip of his pencil against the legal pad. "You know, the police have some theories about why you may have wanted that much money."

Robby crosses his arms and shrugs. "I'm sure they do."

"They think that you owed somebody a lot of money, and that you protected that person's identity after you were arrested."

Robby looks at the blinds, squeezing the armrests in his hands.

"They also have this other theory that maybe you learned about a large stash of Oxy and that you planned to buy it...and maybe start dealing yourself."

He looks back at him. "Well, they're wrong."

The therapist nods and then sets his legal pad on the coffee table. He smiles resignedly. Setting both feet on the floor, he leans forward toward Robby. "You know, anything you say in this room is said in the strictest confidence. I don't report any aspect of our conversation to the police. The only thing that they will know from me is that you are willingly participating in the counseling."

Robby shrugs. "I know."

"Well then, what I need from you is honesty. The therapy won't be nearly as effective if you aren't one hundred percent honest with me."

Robby leans back into his seat, crossing his arms tightly against his chest. "Okay."

The therapist leans back too, crossing his legs again. He smiles genuinely. "So, do you think you might want to tell me why you felt you needed the windfall of money that would have come from selling all of that painting equipment?"

He leans the back of his head into the seat and looks up into the ceiling. He sighs and then slowly looks down into the therapist's eyes. "I just did tell you. I needed money because I was jonesing. I wasn't thinking straight. That's all it was. Honest."

The therapist smiles a tight grin and nods his head. He retrieves his legal pad from the coffee table. "Okay. Then we don't need to talk about that anymore. Thank you." He holds his pencil ready against the paper. "Can I ask you if you've had any urges since getting back?"

Robby rubs a finger slowly up and down the bridge of his nose. He looks at the therapist and flips his hair out of his eyes. "I'd be lying if I said no." He smiles. "And I certainly would never lie to you."

Not taking the bait, the therapist nods, but doesn't write anything. "Have you seen anybody that you used to associate with drug use?"

Robby shakes his head. "Nope. P.P.T," he quotes. "Avoid the people, places, and things that could trigger a relapse."

The therapist smiles. "That's good. I know the letters and the sayings can sound corny, but they can help you remember what you need to do."

"Whatever."

The therapist looks at the ground and then back into Robby's eyes. "Can you tell me what has triggered any recent cravings?"

He rubs his palms together. "Shit, stress, I guess...things not working out the way I want them to."

The therapist jots something down. "You mean with Tiffany and then with your old boss?"

Robby crosses his arms. "Yeah."

After a moment, he looks up from the legal pad and smiles.

"Has anything good happened? Have you accomplished anything that you've wanted to accomplish since coming home…even something relatively small?"

He shrugs. "I got a job."

"Good. Good." He writes.

"It's a minimum wage job at a grocery store."

The therapist smiles. "But you accomplished something. You went to an interview, and a stranger saw something good in you, something worth hiring. That's maybe bigger than you're giving it credit as being."

Robby takes a breath and exhales. "I guess."

"Really, you should write it on a piece of paper and tape the piece of paper on a wall where you'll see it when you wake up in the morning. At the end of every day, write some accomplishment on it, even if you simply write, 'I stayed clean today.' When you fill the paper up, tape a blank piece next to it and fill that one. You'll see pretty quickly that you're accomplishing things every day… things worth celebrating. That can help offset the disappointments."

Robby rolls his eyes.

"I know, I know, but I've had people tell me that their list of accomplishments made a bigger difference than they thought that it would. We get a lot more done in a day than we think, but it's human nature to focus on what we didn't get done. If you dwell too much on your perceived failures, it can drag you down, and that can trigger cravings."

Robby laces his fingers in front of his face and touches his lips against the tips of his thumbs. He nods thoughtfully. "I guess that makes sense."

"It's not enough to just think about those accomplishments. Seeing them in writing…that can often have a much more profound effect." He makes a note on his pad. "Writing in general can play a big role in your recovery. I'm sure they mentioned keeping a journal at New Sunrises."

"They required it."

The therapist nods. "Are you still keeping one now?"

"No. That didn't really do anything for me. It just made me frustrated." He flicks a finger into the palm of his other hand. "I don't like to write like that."

The therapist tilts his head and nods. "Well, not everything we recommend will work for you. You have to experiment. Will you at least try the list I mentioned? It doesn't take much writing."

Robby shrugs. "Yeah, I'll try it."

He jots. "Good. Thank you. I think it might really mean something to you." He smiles. "And congratulations on the new job. Finding employment is often one of the biggest challenges for people in recovery, so you jumped a major hurdle. That's great."

Robby smiles faintly and looks toward the blinds again.

"Besides the group work and the one-on-one therapy was there anything else at New Sunrises that was helpful for you?"

Robby shrugs. "They had a punching bag in the gym. I worked out on that nearly every day."

The therapist bobs his head up and down. "Did your counselor have you visualize the bag as your addiction?"

He laughs. "No, it wasn't part of my therapy or anything. I just did it myself. It was a good workout."

"Gotcha." He smiles. "Was it a speed bag?"

He shakes his head. "No, a heavy bag."

"Do you have one at home you can use?"

"No."

The therapist jots something in his notes. "So, right now, what are you doing to cope when you do have a craving?"

Robby shrugs. "Mostly listening to music."

The therapist scratches down a few words. "Does it help?"

"I've always been able to get lost in music. It takes my mind off things pretty quickly."

"That's excellent. You already have a tool that's working for you." He sets the pencil in his lap and steeples his fingertips against each other. "Another thing you can do is focus on the consequences. Don't think about how good it would feel to be high. Think instead about the negative things that using brought to your life. Think about how you'd feel about yourself afterwards. Think about what Tiffany or your mom or your old boss would think if they saw you using again."

Robby rests his forehead against his palm and looks at the floor.

"I know that sounds harsh, but thinking about the consequences can be a powerful motivator to keep you from slipping back into the behaviors that made you a person that you don't want to be. Right?"

Robby doesn't look up, but nods his head. A tear falls between his legs and disappears into the carpet.

The therapist is quiet. Then, he clears his throat. "Do you have a sponsor?"

Not looking up, he shakes his head.

"Well, it's not an integral part of the program that you're in. Still, it is an option. It gives you someone to talk to who has been through what you're going through." He waits for Robby to look up. "Do you think that you would like a sponsor?"

"Not really."

The therapist nods. "Fair enough. You have that emergency number if you ever really need to talk with someone without fear of judgment. Nevertheless, talking with someone who has been through addiction can be different than speaking with someone on a hotline. It can allow you to be more open than—"

"I don't want a sponsor."

The therapist nods and then writes something down. He looks up from his pages. "Well, with the time we have left, I'd like to talk about the history of your addiction. Would that be okay?"

Robby shrugs. "That's fine. Whatever."

The therapist smiles. "How is it that you started using Oxy?"

He blinks and then looks at a folder sitting on the side table next to the therapist's chair. He motions his head toward it. "Isn't that all in my file?"

"A version of it, yes. But, I want to hear your version in your own words."

Robby sits up and leans back into the chair. He stuffs his hands into the pockets of his hoodie. "Not much to the story, really. Not last October, but the October before that I was working for a roofing company. I fell off a ladder and hurt my back. My doctor had me on OxyContin at first when the pain was really bad. Friends came over and showed me how to break the pills into powder and snort them. It was pretty much downhill from there."

"Friends?"

Robby nods. "Guys from a band I used to be in."

The therapist picks up his pad and writes. "Do you still see these friends?"

"No. Two of them are in Kalamazoo. I haven't talked to them in over a year. And Duffy, our lead singer, is in seminary school."

"Seminary?"

He nods. "Duffy never touched the Oxy. He just drank now and again. Not much of that, either. He was always pretty straight-laced."

The therapist re-crosses his legs. "How long did the doctor have you on the medication?"

"He didn't want it to be for very long, but I was lying to him about the pain. It wasn't until January that he said he wanted to try to switch me over to Tylenol." He shrugs. "It didn't matter by then because I'd already found a way to get the stuff without a prescription."

A telephone rings in another room somewhere in the building.

"This might be counter-productive to what I said earlier, but what did you enjoy about being high?"

Robby looks at the floor again. He moves a fingertip in a small circle on his thigh. "I don't know, man. I felt good. Pure happy, you know? It let me check out of everything. Near the end, I was using it to nod pretty much every night."

The phone stops ringing.

The sound of the therapist's pencil on paper scratches through the room. "Tell me more about your band."

He looks up. "Not much to tell, really. It was more of a high school thing. We played at a lot of parties. Covers, mainly. We worked on a few originals, but we never really could agree on a sound. After high school, Duffy moved away, and Marco was working 50 to 60 hours a week for his old man." He looks at the blinds and shrugs. "It just kind of drifted away."

"Did you like it…playing music?"

Robby looks at him. "I loved it more than anything."

The therapist makes a note. "And do you still play?"

He crosses his arms and shrugs. "Bass isn't all that much fun to play by yourself."

"What about trying to find another band? From what I understand, bass players are hard to come by. Something like that could give you—"

"I sold all my shit."

The therapist holds the pencil up to his eyes, looks at the tip, and then looks at Robby. "For drug money?"

Robby exhales a deep breath and nods.

The therapist writes. "Where were you living during all of this? I mean, after your back injury?"

"My mom's."

"Were you working?"

"No."

"Do you think she had any idea that you had a problem?"

Robby laces his fingers, stretches his hands above his head, and cracks his knuckles. He speaks through his moan. "She just thought that I had a motivation problem. She was pretty cool about me staying there. I told her that my plan was to go to O.C.C. in the fall, and she said that as long as that was my plan I could stay there for free."

"That's Oakland Community College, right?"

"Yup."

The therapist makes note of it. "Was that your plan?"

He scratches his wrist. "My plan was to stay high as often as I could."

The therapist cups his left hand over his right fist and rests both against his lips. He talks into them. "So, when you were selling all of your things, you told her that you were putting money away for college."

"Exactly."

He nods, picking up his pencil and pad again from his lap. He flips it to a fresh page. "How did you end up working for Ty?"

Robby sighs. "A guy I knew from high school was working for him. He said that Ty was looking for guys, so I went and talked to him. Why is any of this—"

"This was in…?"

"April."

He writes and then looks up. "Did you tell your mom that you were saving the money from work for school?"

"Yup."

He clears his throat. "How did you feel about lying to her?"

"I wasn't really feeling much of anything."

"How do you feel about it now?"

Robby smirks at him. "Shitty. What do you think?"

"Did you end up going to O.C.C.?"

"No."

"Because of money?"

"I just didn't."

"And your mother didn't have an issue—"

"She was just happy that I was still working for Ty...that I was sticking with something. I told her that I'd go to school in the winter. Ty only does exterior stuff, so I'd be more freed up in the winter. Look, this is—"

"But then you stole his equipment."

Robby digs his nails into the arm of the chair. "You know all this crap. Why do we have to keep talking about it?"

"It makes you feel bad?"

"No shit."

The therapist motions his pencil eraser at him. "I know this seems pointless, but it's important for you to be in touch with these emotions. I want you to remember how you feel right now...for when you have a craving."

Robby looks into his lap. "I don't need any help to feel shitty about myself. I've got that covered."

"Just remember that it can be a useful emotion."

He shrugs.

The therapist flips through the pages that he's written on, reading here and there. "You said that using allowed you to 'check out.' What exactly were you trying to escape while getting high?"

Robby sits quietly studying the therapist. Then, he sighs. "Everything. I mean, the band had fallen apart. I didn't really know what I was doing with my life." He flips his hands into the air in front of him. "Shit like that, I guess."

"Had the band already broken up by the time you hurt your back?"

Robby nods. "About six months before. We didn't really do anything official. We just sort of stopped practicing…stopped playing."

"But you still spent time together?"

"Some of us. We were friends, still."

He nods and then writes on his pad. "Was it still that painful for you…six months later?"

He shrugs his palms into the air, fingers splayed. "It wasn't any one thing. I mean, the Cotton just made me feel really good."

"It can be a powerful drug."

"Damn straight."

The therapist flips back to his first sheet and reads. Then, "And what about Tiffany?"

He adjusts himself in his seat. "What about her?"

"You said that you had feelings for her in high school. Did you ever act on them?"

"I couldn't. She was Mikey's girl. They were together for a year and a half. They broke up at the end of our junior year."

"And then?"

"And then, nothing." He shrugs one shoulder. "Her mom moved over the summer, and the next year she was at a different high school. I didn't see her anymore."

"Until that party."

After a moment, he nods.

"And then she reciprocated your feelings."

"You could say that."

He flips back to the most recent page he'd written on. "Before then, you'd never let her know how you felt?"

"No."

"Why not?"

He grunts a laugh. "Because Mikey probably would have killed me."

The therapist scribbles something down. "How would you say your feelings for her developed?"

Robby repeatedly flicks the middle finger of his right hand into his left palm. "I don't know. We talked all the time. She came to all of our practices. The other guys smoked, and when they'd go outside, me and her talked." He shrugs. "She was cool."

"You didn't smoke?"

He shakes his head.

"What did you talk about with Tiffany?" he asks while jotting something down.

"I don't know...all kinds of shit."

"Would you say that you talked with her about things that you didn't talk about with other people?"

He scratches a finger into the cleft of his chin. "Probably."

"Like what?"

"I can't remember right now. We just talked, okay?"

"That's fine." The therapist glances over his page. "Do you smoke cigarettes now?"

Robby squeezes his arms tighter against his chest. "No. I never got into it."

"But you tried them?"

"A few times. They tasted like shit. I didn't understand the fascination."

The therapist nods thoughtfully. "That's really actually quite uncommon. A majority of people who've had problems with drugs tend to be smokers." He taps his pencil against his legal pad. "I've always taken that as a good sign when a recovering addict isn't a smoker. I don't have anything conclusive, but I've always taken that to mean that you don't have a naturally addictive personality. It's very interesting in your case because you spent time with smokers. The guys in your band...they smoked a lot?"

"Like fiends."

The therapist works his thumb over the eraser of his pencil. "What about at New Sunrises? Were your fellow patients smokers?"

"Holy shit, yes."

"And I would imagine that they offered you cigarettes."

He nods. "It's like some of them were pissed at me that I didn't smoke. They started calling me Pink."

"Pink?"

"For pink lungs, I guess. A lot of those guys were assholes."

The therapist smiles sympathetically. "Did that make it difficult for you to form friendships there?"

"I didn't care about making friends there."

He writes on his pad. "What I'm hearing gives me high hopes for you, Robby. Very high hopes. You have a perseverant personality. You don't seem naturally inclined to addiction, which should make your recovery that much more likely to be successful."

He grins. "So you're saying that I don't have to come here anymore?"

The therapist chuckles. "Not exactly. I'm simply saying that I'm very optimistic." He flips to a fresh page in his notebook. "I do, however, have one more question for you."

"Shoot."

"Do you feel that in recounting the last couple of years to me that you may have inadvertently left something out?"

Robby drums his fingers on the arms of his chair. "Not that I can think of. I told you that I'm not lying to you."

"I know." He reaches for Robby's file and flips through its contents. "Didn't something else happen that might account for your feelings of wanting to escape?"

Robby's face goes grim. He crosses his arms and stares into his lap. "No."

The therapist looks at the pages in the open file. "The end of last summer. No, not last summer...the summer before. Your father's tragic... What I mean is that your file says that your father took his own—"

"Isn't our time up?"

The therapist looks at his watch. "I suppose it is." He taps his finger on the watch, and his face looks thoughtful. "I don't have anyone scheduled until after lunch though, so if you'd like to keep—"

He doesn't look up from his lap. "No. I'm ready to be done. I've got shit to do."

"Okay." He flips the legal pad back to the first page and then sets it on the table. "We can begin next time where we left off today."

"Whatever. I don't fucking care."

"I do have some homework for you, though." He smiles encouragingly. "I'd like you to start keeping that daily list of accomplishments. Will you do that?"

"Maybe."

The therapist nods. "I'll take 'maybe.' And I appreciate your honesty about it."

Robby stands and flips his hood up over his head. "Can I go?"

The therapist stands and motions towards his seat. "You seem a little upset right now. I'd rather not end the session this way."

He crosses his arms. "I need to go. I'm fine."

The therapist rubs his palm over one cheek and then the other. "A suicide like that can leave a significant hole of unanswered questions. We can begin to fill that hole with things that aren't necessarily true. We begin to think about how we might be to blame for—"

He turns.

"Robby." The therapist starts after him.

"Fuck this, man. I'm out." Robby bolts through the doorway and slams the door closed between them.

~*~

Watching his feet, Robby threads his way through the grave markers in Plymouth's Riverside Cemetery. He stops, looks around, and then alters his direction, angling toward a small mausoleum with black pillars and an ornate steel door. The tall pines around him cast long shadows eastward across the lawn. He stuffs his hands deep into the pockets of his hoodie, glancing at and reading the names that he passes. He looks at the crosses and the occasional stars of David. In the distance, a woman stands from kneeling, crosses herself, and then walks away from a gravesite. Robby watches her.

~*~

Not far from a copse of birch trees, Robby stops in front of a granite headstone. The face of it is hazy with dried rainwater, dust, and weeks-old pollen. White streaks run from the top to the bottom of the stone.

He looks at the name: Gerald Cooper.

"Hey, Dad," he whispers.

After a moment, he sits crossed-legged on the grass in front of the headstone. He looks at his pretzeled legs. "Sit on your biscuits," he mumbles and then smiles to himself absently.

Using the sleeve of his hoodie like a rag, he leans forward and rubs some of the grime from the headstone. He leans back and looks at it.

Elbow propped on his thigh and hand covering his mouth, he stares at his father's name. His finger moves slowly on his upper lip. "Sorry Dad," he mouths. After a moment, he averts his eyes to the ground. He shivers in a breeze that blows across the grass.

Entering from the north, a line of cars weaves gradually through the cemetery following the curving road. The lead car is a long, black hearse followed by other sedans. A small orange flag shimmies on the hood of each.

Robby watches them until they go out of sight behind a row of evergreens.

Looking across the stretch of lawn and headstones, he waits. The cars appear again. The lead car pulls slowly to the side onto the grass. Keeping behind the hearse, the others begin parking on either side of the road.

Robby pats his pocket and then reaches in, pulling out his phone. He twirls it slowly between his thumb and fingers. Across the cemetery, men in dark suits and women in dark dresses emerge from the doors of the cars. A few children follow the adults, looking unsure how to behave.

A man opens the back doors of the hearse.

Robby scrolls through his contacts, stops on a name, and hits send. The phone on the other end rings three times, and then someone picks up.

"Hey, Robby."

"You answered."

Tiffany is quiet on her end. Then, "Yeah, I answered. Why are you calling?"

He clears his throat. "No reason, really. It's just been awhile since we talked."

"It's been three weeks."

He shrugs. "That's awhile."

"Is it?"

The pallbearers lift an end of the casket and roll it slowly forward.

"Is it okay that I called? Can you talk?"

She waits a moment. "Yeah, I can talk."

"How have things been?" He flips his hair from his eyes.

She inhales. "Good. Really busy, though. The doctor has me coming in every other week."

"Is something wrong?"

"No. Just getting closer to my delivery date."

He switches the phone to his other ear, watching the pallbearers. Clouds shift over the sun, and the shadows of the trees disappear. "Did you get that box I left at your apartment?"

"I did." She laughs. "I won't be able to use those diapers you bought until next Christmas."

He scratches his eyebrow. "Why?"

"Didn't you even read the package?"

"Not really."

"Robby. Babies aren't 27 pounds when they come out."

He rips up a handful of grass and then sprinkles the blades back onto the ground. "I didn't know. There was a picture of a baby on the package."

She laughs again. "Newborns usually aren't able to sit up on their own."

"Well, I don't know, what do I know about babies?"

"Not much, obviously," she says, laughing again.

"Obviously." He pulls up another handful of grass and sprinkles it into his lap. "You can still use them though, right?"

"Yes, I can use them," she says. "Eventually."

He waits a moment. "You're not mad?"

In the distance, the pallbearers walk the casket away from the hearse. One woman is guided behind them by a friend walking with a hand on each of her shoulders. She looks as though without the help she would fall onto the ground.

"No, I'm not mad."

"It was just a spur of the moment kind of thing. I saw the diapers in the store, and I bought them."

"That was nice. Thanks."

He reaches into his pocket and pulls out a folded piece of paper.

"So, are you working?" she asks.

He shakes the paper open. It's a printed page from a website. It's a list of questions. "Just a bag boy job at a grocery."

"Oh man, that can't be very fun."

He reads some of the questions on the paper to himself. "It's not all bad. It's busy, so the day goes by pretty fast." He sniffs. "And, I heard something might open up on the overnight stocking shift, too. If that happens and I get it, that's a buck more an hour."

"That'd be good." She's quiet a moment. "Are you thinking at all about taking any classes next—"

"Hey, Tif, can I ask you something?"

Silence. Then, "I don't know. What is it?"

His eyes move over the paper and then stop. "Do you...do you believe that each life has a purpose?" he asks, half reading and half speaking.

"What?"

"A purpose. Do you think our lives have a specific purpose, like each person's life?"

"A purpose?"

"Yeah, like you. What is Tiffany Whiting's purpose in your eyes? What were you meant for?"

She laughs nervously. "Robby, what are you...? I don't know how to answer that. My purpose? God, I don't know. I'm not even sure if I want to know. It's probably depressing, like my purpose is to make other people feel better about their lives."

"Don't say that."

"Well, then, I don't know. I don't know what to say."

"That's okay. You don't have to answer. I was just..." He looks at the paper again. "Well, what about this? What's one of the biggest things that your life has taught you so far?"

She laughs again. "Where are you coming up with these questions?"

"I don't know." He crumples up the paper in his fist. "You used to come up with questions like that for me all the time in high school. Really deep, you know?"

"I did?" She is quiet a moment. "I guess I did. Wow. Off the top of my head, I can't come up with some big life lesson that I've learned. That's kinda sad. Did I use to have answers back in high school?"

He squeezes the ball of paper. "I don't know. You were usually asking me the questions."

She laughs. "That was one of my talents...getting other people to talk. I even thought about going into social work at one time."

He doesn't say anything, squeezing the ball tighter.

"Soon as I got the job at Shuette's, though, that was that." She sighs. "I never did sign up for classes."

He releases pressure on the crumpled paper. "That's why you didn't go to school...because of the job at the dealership?"

"Pretty much. At the time, what they were paying me didn't seem too bad. It didn't feel like I needed to go to school, you know?"

He nods. "Yeah."

"After about a year with my apartment and my car payment, the idea of going back to school seemed like a dream."

He tosses the paper into the air and catches it. "I suppose you're right...about questions like that, I mean. You know, about life. They were just a game back then...something to talk about. Nothing on the line. But now, coming up with an answer feels like a lot more pressure...like you want to hear yourself say something kinda important, like you actually know something."

"Why? You don't know what Robby Cooper's purpose is?" She laughs good-naturedly.

"Oh, hell no." He pauses. "Disappointing people, I guess."

"Don't say that..."

The woman who had needed help walking breaks away from the mourners and collapses sobbing on the trunk of a Cadillac behind the hearse. A blonde woman follows and then embraces her. Robby watches.

"People can always surprise you," Tiffany says.

He blinks. "What?"

"That'd be my answer to your last question...about the biggest thing my life has taught me so far."

The blonde woman opens the back door to the Cadillac and ushers the crying woman inside.

Watching the women, he swallows. "Who has surprised you?"

"Well, my mom, for one. Back in high school, it seemed like she wanted nothing to do with me, like she wished I wasn't even around. I don't know, I guess she was still dealing with the pain of my dad leaving her." Tiffany is quiet a moment. "Now she calls me every day. I know it's a lot to do with the baby, but I didn't know that she had it in her to be so concerned about me, you know? I thought that when I told her that I was pregnant it was going to push her even further away. It's weird, though. It's like she's not disappointed in me at all. It's like she's happy or something."

Robby throws the paper into the air and catches it again. "Are you letting her help?"

"A little. She came over this past weekend and helped me paint the room that I'm going to use as the nursery. She's not after me anymore to move back in with her either, like she understands why I want to do this on my own. That makes a big difference...that she's not telling me anymore why it's silly for me not to just move back home."

"That's cool."

"It's so weird. While we were painting, we talked the whole time." She laughs. "There were times in high school that a week would go by and we might say ten words to each other. If that. I don't get it. It's like she's a different person."

He nods. "My mom has been pretty cool with my situation, too. She's trying a little too hard to be helpful, but she's trying. I know she could be treating me a lot worse if she wanted. She never makes me feel bad for everything I put everyone through."

Off by a tree, one of the mourners lights a cigarette. Most of the others watch the Cadillac intently.

"You know," Tiffany starts, "I think I do believe that everyone has a purpose. I mean, we're each meant for something, you know? Some people just don't find it or get side-tracked, I guess."

Robby looks away from the mourners toward his father's headstone. He rubs his fingers on his temple. "I haven't met that many people who aren't sidetracked."

"What about Duffy?"

Tilting his head to the side, he rubs his fingertips over his cheek. "That's true." He laughs. "Of course, Mikey always said that Duffy only wanted to go to seminary so he could shack up with other closet homos like him."

"Mikey was an asshole."

Robby doesn't respond.

"Mikey was always jealous of Duffy," she says. "I think it bothered him to be around somebody that knew exactly what he wanted to do and was just waiting for the time to come to do it." She pauses. "I remember Duffy talking about seminary even back in ninth grade. Nobody from his family was really religious or anything. He just knew that's what he wanted to do."

Robby shakes his head. "Man, when Mikey would get drunk, he'd go after Duffy all the time…get right in his face, yelling about how Duffy was breaking up the band with his seminary bullshit. He even popped him once right in the mouth. Duffy just walked away." He looks toward the mourners. The woman who had been crying stands up out of the open car door. She nods her head determinedly to something the blonde woman says. "We never played together again after that," Robby says. "The band was done after that."

"Mikey punched Duffy?"

"Loosened a couple of his teeth from what I remember."

"God," she says. "Such an asshole."

"You're the one who dated him." He winces after he says it and shakes his head.

"Don't remind me."

He squeezes the ball of paper. "Why did you stay with him for so long, anyway? Seemed like you guys were always fighting about something."

"Why does anybody do anything in high school? I probably stayed with him because my mom hated him so much." She breathes and then exhales through her nose into the mouthpiece of the phone. "He wasn't always bad, either. When nobody else was around, he could be sweet. He was really... I don't know, vulnerable, I guess. He was so jealous of everybody."

"He could be all right most of the time," Robby says. "He wasn't too bad toward me."

"Maybe, but he was jealous of you, too."

"Of me?"

"Yeah. It always made him angry that you were so good at coming up with lyrics."

He laughs. "The stuff Mikey wrote was pretty terrible. Jesus that one song... 'Rock the Weekend'? He actually rhymed cocaine with Rogaine."

"It's sad, too, because he wanted so bad for it to be good. He worked on those stupid songs for days. He'd even sing them to me. He wanted to be a good singer, too. That's another reason he was jealous of Duffy."

"No doubt about it, Duffy could sing." He looks at two robins around the base of an evergreen. One of the birds bounces in circles around the other. "You think he's still in seminary?"

"I don't know. I hope so," she says. "I like the idea that he's still there, you know? It's like one of us made it."

"I should call him sometime...at least call his mom's place." Robby pulls up another handful of grass. "I really should. I always liked Duffy." He wiggles his pinky and ring finger and watches the blades of grass funnel out the bottom of his hand sprinkling onto the ground. "I bet you'll be a really great mom, Tif."

She makes a small hum in her throat. "Thanks, Robby. I hope I am. I guess that would be a pretty good purpose."

"It'd be a great one."

"I think that was half of Mikey's problem. His dad was terrible to him."

"He was?"

"He didn't really talk about it," she says, "but his dad ran him down all the time. I remember we were sitting on their couch once, and his dad came in and said, 'You seem like a girl with her head on. Why would you date a worthless loser like him?'"

Robby shakes his head. "Man."

"I know, right? I didn't know what to say. I laughed because I thought he had to be joking. He didn't laugh, though. He shook his head and said, 'It's not funny. You just wait. He's going to be a big let-down for you.' He stared at Mikey for a second and then he walked out of the room."

"Did Mikey say anything?"

"He said he had to get something out of his room. He came back about fifteen minutes later, and his eyes were all red. I tried to ask him if he was all right, but he just said that he wanted to go to a movie, so we went to a movie. After the movie, he seemed fine. We'd only been dating a couple months, so I didn't ask him too much about it. Later he started telling me more stories about his dad and things he would say. The guy was really toxic."

Robby touches his finger along the bridge of his nose. "I had no idea."

"Like I said, Mikey really didn't talk about it except with me sometimes. I think that's part of why I stayed with him, too... because I felt sorry for him."

"I can see that."

The robins fly away.

"But you can only feel sorry for someone for so long," she says. "Mikey eventually started being mean to me the way his dad was mean to him. I could see that, but he couldn't. I'd even tell him that, but it'd just make him meaner. It was like he lived for all that anger...like he craved it or something."

Robby nods. "He was really angry about the band splitting up. I'd never seem him like I saw him that night. After what he did to Duffy, we all took off. He seemed ready to go after anyone."

"Being in that band was everything to him...especially when you guys started to get a bit of a following."

He rubs his fingers on his forehead and looks at the ground. "I guess I can kind of see why it meant so much to him. It meant a lot to me, too."

"That still didn't give him the right to act that way, you know? I even tried to get him to see that his dad was the loser, not him. He wouldn't listen. He was choosing to be miserable."

Robby stands up and slaps his hand against his pant leg. He stuffs the wad of paper into the pocket of his hoodie and looks at his father's name etched in the stone. "I've been thinking a lot about my dad lately."

She's quiet for a moment. "I feel really bad that I didn't call you after he...after I heard what happened."

He shrugs. "It's okay. It'd been a long time since we'd talked." He sees the mourners gathered around the gravesite looking toward the pastor. The murmur of his words comes across the distance, indecipherable but cadenced.

"That must have been really hard."

He walks slowly toward the mourners. "It's funny. I was supposed to be one of the pallbearers at my dad's funeral. I lied, though, and told my mom that I screwed up my back skateboarding and that I couldn't do it. They got one of my cousins to take my place." He shakes his head. "I don't know why I lied. Isn't that fucked up?"

"I don't think you should look back on stuff like that too much. It doesn't really do any good."

He sniffs in a wet breath through his nose and pushes the back of his hand through his eyes. "That's all I've been doing lately, you know? I keep thinking about all my mistakes."

A little boy runs from the mourners but returns after a sharp word from what appears to be his father.

"Robby, I think I should probably get going," Tiffany says.

He nods. "Okay. Do you mind, though... I mean, would it be all right if I call you again sometime?"

A moment passes. "I don't mind," she says.

"Okay. I won't abuse it or anything. Just sometime I might call again. Or maybe I won't. You can call me too if you ever want to."

"All right. Bye, Robby."

"Bye."

He keeps walking.

~*~

He stands at the edge of the line of parked mourners' cars. He listens to the words he can catch from the pastor. "Taken too soon…a mystery not…eases our burden no less…"

He crosses between the cars, crosses the road, and then crosses between the cars on the other side. The mourners' heads are bowed. He leans against a pine tree some fifty feet from the casket where it sits on the platform that will lower it into the ground. His hair hangs in his eyes. The pastor is reading from a book.

"…body that is sown is perishable, it is raised imperishable; it is sown in dishonor, it is raised in glory; it is sown in weakness, it is raised in power; it is sown a natural body, it is raised a spiritual body." The pastor clears his throat and then continues reading. "If there is a natural body, there is also a spiritual body. So it is written: 'The first man Adam became a living being'; the last Adam, a life-giving spirit. The spiritual did not come first, but the natural, and after the spiritual. The first man was of the dust of the earth, the second man from heaven. As was the earthly man, so shall we bear the likeness of the man from heaven. I declare to you, brothers, that flesh and blood cannot inherit the kingdom of God, nor does the perishable inherit the imperishable. Listen, I tell you a mystery: We will not all sleep, but we will all be changed— in a flash, in the twinkling of an eye, at the last—"

The woman who had cried looks up. She turns her head toward Robby and squints in his direction.

He shivers. Averting his eyes, he peels himself from the tree and walks briskly toward his car.

"'Where O death is your victory?'"

Robby walks into his bedroom and then closes the door. A *Return of the Jedi* comforter is draped across his bed. On the walls are posters of Geddy Lee, Flea, John Entwistle, and Les Claypool. He reaches into his pocket, takes out the pill container, and sets it on top of the desk near the window. He studies it for a moment before sitting down in the chair. The darkness outside and the light inside make a mirror of the window in front of him. He looks at his reflection and brushes his hair away from his face. He picks up the container and turns it slowly between thumb and finger.

A knock comes from the door behind him.

"Robby?"

He sets the container down and flings it across the surface. It falls behind the desk and pings metallic against the radiator.

"Can I come in?"

He turns the chair away from the desk. "Yeah."

His mother opens the door and, finding him with her gaze, smiles encouragingly. She wears a fleece jacket over a t-shirt and faded jeans. Her hair is piled into a loose bun on top of her head. "I didn't hear you come home. I was in the backyard on the phone with Aunt Cindy. It's a nice night, but I think it might rain."

He nods.

She takes a few steps into the room. "What are you doing up here?"

"It's my room, Mom. I'm sitting in my room."

She looks around at the posters and then looks at him. "Sitting at your desk?"

He smiles. "Can't get anything past you."

She looks at the desk. Her face softens. "When you were little, I remember you'd get home from school and run right up here." She shakes her head. "I never had to tell you to get to your homework. You were always on it first thing. You really loved school."

He looks at the floor. "I don't remember."

"You were an easy kid…easy baby too. You always slept five or six hours through the night, even when we first brought you home. I remember—"

"Mom? Do you need something?"

She looks at him. "What? No. I just came up to say hello."

He nods. "Okay. Hello. I'm getting ready to go out, so I don't have a lot of time."

She takes a step back, touching her fingers along her cheek until they stop on her lips. "You're going out?"

"Just to a movie."

She smiles. "Do you want company?"

He grins thinly. "No, not really. It's a horror thing, anyway. You wouldn't like it."

"Well, I don't know. I'm getting braver when it comes to that stuff. Netflix had that Blair Witch thing, and I—"

"Mom, I'm just going to go by myself."

She nods slowly. "Okay, honey. Have a good time." She turns toward the door.

"Mom?"

"Yes?"

"Your hair looks good like that. You should wear it up like that more often."

She reaches up and touches the bun. "This? I just pulled it up like this after work."

He swivels the chair back to the desk. "Well, it looks good. It's pretty."

She's quiet a moment. "Thanks," she says. She closes the door behind her.

Robby sits looking at his reflection in the glass. Then, he pushes back the chair and crawls under the desk. His hand gropes in the dark along the floor near the radiator.

~*~

Robby fills a second plastic cup from the keg and then turns and threads his way through the wall of people in the kitchen. Bass from Pearl Jam's "Even Flow" is like a heartbeat in the air around them. The song is close to done. Robby nudges a guy with his elbow, and the guy leans forward to make room for him to pass.

"Thanks," he shouts.

"No problem."

A stratosphere of cigarette smoke hangs above the talking and laughing heads. He holds the cups in the air to keep from spilling as people jostle into him.

The living room is no less crammed or smoky. He turns to the side and edges his way through the bodies. Nickleback's "Photograph" starts through the speakers, and a couch full of girls starts to sing along, loud and off-key.

He rolls his eyes and snaps his bangs from his face.

"Turn this shit off!" someone shouts.

The girls sing louder.

A guy wearing a Detroit Rugby Football Club sweatshirt steps up onto the coffee table and walks across it toward the kitchen. He spills a few beers and an ashtray of butts.

"Hey man!"

He stops in the middle of the table and looks. "Yeah?"

"Nothing."

Near the front window, a guy with long blonde hair pulled back into a ponytail looks up from his phone and makes eye contact with Robby. He toasts his cup toward him. Robby bows his head as greeting. "Hey," he mouths.

"Robby dog!"

Robby smiles and motions his head toward a doorway that leads out of the living room. Ponytail nods, holds up a finger, and then looks at his phone again.

~*~

Robby taps a bedroom door with his foot. A guy wearing sunglasses and with tattoos sleeved up both arms opens the door and looks at him.

"Robby," he says, dragging out his name.

"Andy," Robby says in return.

Andy lets him into the room and then closes the door. Six or seven people sit on the floor smoking cigarettes and blowing smoke toward the open window. Their fingers slide or tap on the screens of their phones. They text. The rain is a faint whisper out in the darkness. Robby steps through the obstacle course of legs and cups. He hands a beer to a guy wearing a Deep Purple t-shirt and then sits on the bed next to him.

"Thanks, Robby my man."

"No problem."

Someone knocks shave-and-a-hair-cut on the door. Andy gets up and opens it. The guy with the ponytail from the living room stands in the doorway craning his neck into the room. "Blister in the Sun" by the Violent Femmes blares behind him.

"Hey, Chris. What's up?" Andy shouts.

"Andy dog," Chris says, smiling while closing the door. He looks at the guy sitting next to Robby on the bed. "Shane, your house is crawling with Comets."

"Hey," Shane says, "talk to Cody. He's the one that likes to over-charge the high school kids for drinking off the keg."

A skinny, red-headed girl wearing all black blows a snake of smoke up into the air above them. "And you're the one that sleeps with them."

"Fuck you," Shane says. "It was one time, and I was in no condition to judge the morality of the situation. Way I was feeling, I couldn't tell the difference between 14 and 40."

"She was 14, dude?"

"No... I just meant—"

The red-head takes a drag of her cigarette. "Shane likes his women to have the smell of Junior prom on them."

"Yeah, yeah, yeah. Get the hell out of my room if you don't like the company, Lisa."

Lisa leans toward the window, exhales, and then sits again. She picks up her phone and scans the screen.

"And, look at that," Shane says, "she stays planted on her needful little ass...ethics be damned."

Lisa looks at him and sticks her tongue out from a defeated pout. The others laugh.

"I didn't see Cody," Robby says, snapping his hair from his face. "He around?"

"Down in the basement playing pool. Whole 'nother party down there."

Robby nods, taking a drink from his beer.

"How you been keeping yourself busy, Chris?" Shane asks. "When I saw you over at Twelve Oaks this morning it was the first time I'd seen your sorry ass in months."

"Twelve Oaks!" another of the girls says.

"He was getting something from Claire's for one of his girlfriends," Lisa says. "They like Hello Kitty."

"Ladies," Shane says, "this reverse psychology flirting is getting old…and could get you booted. I'm only so merciful."

The girls smoke sullenly and check their phones.

"I was working for my old man," Chris says.

"Landscaping?"

He nods. "He's got me on hiatus until some more bids come through."

"You looking for other work?"

"Shit man, where?"

Shane slaps Robby on the back and laughs good-naturedly. "Our man here is a big shooter in the staples and dry goods industry. He probably has a bead on several lucrative positions."

Chris looks at Robby with a face both puzzled and hopeful.

Robby looks out from under his fallen hair. "I'm bagging groceries, dude."

Chris smiles and nods. "No shame, man. Gotta do what you gotta do."

"Or," Shane says, "Lisa could probably use a new pimp." He smiles at her quick look. "The pay is infrequent, and you gotta deal with numerous customer complaints, but it's something."

"Fuck you, Shane."

He smiles and pulls one of his pockets inside out. "Sorry, I don't have the dollar."

She flips him the middle finger.

"What about you? What are you doing?" Chris asks, pulling the band on his ponytail tighter and sitting cross-legged on the floor.

Shane shakes his head. "For now, still at Bennigans."

Lisa laughs.

"Quiet," he says, smiling.

Chris tucks a few loose hairs behind his ears. "You almost done with school?"

"More than almost done. I'm done. Graduated in December."

Robby looks at him. "Shit, man, that was fast."

He shrugs. "Didn't feel fast. Went year-round. And now, I am the proud holder of an Associate of Arts in Graphic Design."

Chris raises his cup to him. "Congrats, man. That's cool as shit."

"Actually," Shane says, smiling, "it's just plain shit. I might as well have an Associates in VHS repair."

"What?" one of the girls asks. "What's that?"

"Job hunt isn't going so well?" Chris asks, ignoring her.

Shane laughs. "I wish there was a hunt, man. I can barely find anybody looking for a graphic designer. Or, if they are, they're looking for somebody who already has experience. It's almost like an entry-level position doesn't exist, not around Detroit anyway. I've done some freelance stuff for a place in Germany, but that's about it."

"Man," Chris says, "Since December?"

Shane nods.

"That blows."

"No shit, dude. I was in that program for two years. The whole time you're in it, all you hear is how exciting the field is. Everything was about all the doors that my education would open. They make it seem like you're doing everything right. Then, man, I swear, during that last week of my capstone course, the instructor started getting all gloom and doom. He was telling us that either we needed to learn how to freelance and live hand to mouth or that we should plan on getting at least a bachelor's degree. He said that even that didn't guarantee anything because the market is saturated with designers. He actually said, 'Get a job as a waiter. You're going to need it.'"

He shakes his head. "I had that fucker for three other classes. He never talked like that when he was teaching them. I remember him always saying that what he was trying to do was give us real-world experience. Then, in that last week, he said, 'The real world could care less about your degree. It's all about talent and drive. You've been living in a dream world set at a dream pace. Work at the pace that we set in here, and you'll never get a position or land a project.' He used to make it seem like we'd walk out the door and into a career. The whole thing feels like a snow job, you know?"

The people sitting on the floor ash their cigarettes and stare at the glowing tips. Their phones ding with received texts. Robby glances at a Pink Floyd album cover pinned to Shane's wall.

"That's bullshit, man," Chris says.

Shane takes a drink of his beer and then shakes his head. "They didn't teach us anything about doing freelance. By the time I was done with that Germany project I made less than minimum wage for the hours that I put in."

"Total bullshit."

Shane stares at the floor, nodding. The rain murmurs outside the window. He looks into his cup and tilts it from side to side. Then he gets up and walks over to the window. "Fuck it." He opens the screen and tosses the rest of his beer outside. "Let's get blazed."

"Ah yeah."

~*~

Shane sits back on the bed, leans over Robby, and takes a cigar box from the drawer of his night table. Opening it, he pulls out a bag of marijuana and rolling papers. "If I remember," he says, talking quietly to Robby, "this isn't really your scene."

Those on the floor shift about in grinning anticipation.

Pinching his cup between his knees, Robby scratches his wrist. "Not really. Never much did anything for me."

Shane sprinkles green bud into the fold of a paper. "You being true to your program?"

Robby rests his thumb against his temple and massages his fingers in circles on his forehead. "I guess." He looks at the others' smiling faces. "I don't know. Not really." He scratches his wrist again. "You holding?"

Shane licks the edge of the paper, nodding. "I can set you up with some kicker. You got 40 bones on you?"

Robby crosses his arms and closes his eyes. He opens them after a moment and looks at Shane, nodding. "I got it."

"And you're sure you want it?"

He nods.

Shane tapers the ends of the joint with his licked fingers. "Let me spark this and get it started around…then I'll set you up." He lights the joint and inhales deeply.

The others watch, smiling.

Robby presses his palms together and squeezes his hands between his thighs. He takes a breath and exhales a loud sigh.

Shane hands the joint to Andy. "Enter the kingdom," he says in a tight whisper. A wisp of smoke slips from his lips.

"Ah yeah."

Robby's eyes snap to his lap and he grips his vibrating pocket. Pulling out his phone, he looks at the screen: *Tif*. He jolts to standing. "Holy shit. No way."

Everyone looks at him, heads tilting on their necks.

"I gotta take this, Shane."

He nods. "We'll be here," he says, exhaling a cloud of smoke.

Robby steps through the tire obstacle of crossed legs and beer cups.

"Close the door quick, man. Don't let those Comets smell this stuff," Chris says. "We'll be overrun."

~*~

Robby pushes his way through the barricade of people. Rap music pounds from the stereo.

"Watch it, asshole!"

He presses into the few openings that he can find in the packed room.

"Hey!"

"Slow down, you fuck."

Getting to the screen door, he bursts out onto the porch. "Hello? I'm here. Tif?" He walks down the steps and into the front yard. "Tif?"

"Ro...Robby?"

"Tif? What's wrong?" Holding a hand over his other ear, he walks away from the music into the darkness of the side yard. "Why are you crying?"

She coughs her words. "Someone...someone was in my apartment..."

He stands next to a rectangle of light cast onto the ground from a nearby window. "Someone broke in... Why? What did they take?"

"I don't... I don't know. I can't find anything missing."

"What?"

"There's nothing gone. It's just—"

Robby flips his hood up covering himself against the light rain. "How do you know anyone was there?"

She talks through her crying. "There was a picture of me on my pillow. It was from like ninth grade when I was on the pom squad. It was just…just propped up there."

"A picture?"

"Yeah, right on my pillow. And the scary thing… I mean, that picture was in my closet in a box under other boxes." She cries again. "Someone was in here and they dug through my boxes, Robby. Then they put it all back. Why would someone…why would someone do that?"

"Nothing else was…just that picture?"

"And a rose. There was a rose lying on my counter."

He paces. "A flower…a rose just sitting there?… How did they get in?"

"I don't know. I mean, there's nothing. The front door was locked. The windows…none of the windows were open or broken. I don't… I'm just scared, Robby. It's just really freaking me out."

The door of Shane's house creaks open and then slams shut again.

Tiffany cries.

Robby's hand reaches out to the air in front of him. He brings it back and rubs it over his mouth. "It will be okay. I mean, maybe your Mom…have you talked to your Mom about—"

"I have to go. The police are here. Thanks for picking up, though. I didn't want to sit here and just… I was scared to sit here and think about it, you know?" She sniffles in a long, wet breath.

"Yeah, I can see—"

"I have to go. They're really knocking, okay?"

"Okay. Bye." He hits *end* and watches the screen fade out. Bass reverberates in the house. He looks out into the darkness at the smattering of lit windows around the neighborhood and the silhouettes of trees.

~*~

Fading in through the drizzle and muffled music, jogging footsteps shish across the grass behind him. He starts to turn. A shove sends him sprawling onto the wet ground. Scrambling to his feet, he throws back his hood. "Hey, man. What the fuck?"

A thick outline stands in the darkness. "I thought that was you, Robby."

He swallows. "Mikey?"

"I thought, 'Who's...who's this asshole plowing through the living room like that?'" Mikey lists to his left, catches himself, and then stands straight again. "Then I thought, 'That's fucking Robby. Fucking Robby. Robby's the asshole plowing through.'" He clears his throat and points. "You're the asshole," he slurs.

Robby nibbles the skin along the side of his thumbnail. "I had a phone call."

"I was thinking, 'I can't believe that fucking druggie asshole is here.'" His laugh turns into a cough. "How the hell you doing, Robby boy?"

He swipe-slaps his palms over his wet knees. "Not bad. You been in town long?"

"Fuck you."

Robby looks at a silhouette passing by a window in the house. "Mikey. Come on, man. What's the deal with—"

"Were you fucking her back in high school, too, you little prick?"

He takes a step back. "What? I wasn't—"

Mikey lurches forward and shoves him. "Right there with me, my good friend Robby...fucking my girl every chance he got."

Robby clenches his hands into fists. He shakes his head. "Nothing...nothing ever happened back then, man. You guys were broken up for years before anything happened between us." He shrugs his palms into the air. "You'd already been with Meghan and that other chick from—"

Mikey takes a teetering step forward. He shoves his finger towards Robby's face. "That doesn't mean shit. You're just a lying, little backstabbing fuck."

He holds his hands up. "Come on, man. You're really drunk. Don't start anything. Nothing ever happened between us—"

"She's pregnant, you asshole! You fucking knocked her up. My girl."

"She's not your—"

He lunges forward and Robby back steps outside the range of his grasp. Mikey almost falls but catches himself against the trunk of a tree.

"Take it easy, Mikey. Jesus Christ."

He stumbles away from the tree, raising his fists. "Come on, pussy." Taking a wild, lunging swing, he misses Robby by inches. "Little Robby boy wanted his own cheerleader, so he went after mine."

He stands, clenching his fingernails into his palms. "What did you say?"

"I wanted to marry her. You probably fu...fucked our whole thing. Talking with her like some kind of faggot every chance you got...weaseling in. You fucked it all up."

Robby raises his fists. "It was you, wasn't it, Mikey? The picture on her pillow." He shakes his head. "You scared the shit out of her, man. She's got a fucking kid on the way!"

Mikey rushes forward with his right arm cocked back. Robby ducks the swing and drives a hard jab into his stomach. Mikey drops to his knees, clutching his abdomen and taking gasping breaths.

Robby stands over him, watching him. He wipes the rain from his face.

Mikey leans forward and vomits onto the dark lawn. Falling on his side, he gasps. "Fuck you, Robby."

"You're an asshole, Mikey. You always were." He waits.

Mikey throws up again.

~*~

Sitting in the driver's seat, Robby watches the house. The palm of his right hand slides up and down his left arm. Figures move in the light of the window. Bass pumps the air. A few people stand on the porch smoking cigarettes. Robby licks his lips.

Mikey stumbles from the side yard still clenching his stomach. He hocks back and spits onto the front lawn. After a moment of surveying the street, he stumbles back up the steps and into the party.

"Jesus, Mikey," Robby whispers. "You really let yourself go." He looks at his hand in his lap. Squeezing it into a fist, he turns it back and forth, studying it.

Turning the key in the ignition, he shifts into *drive*. The dashboard glows. On the radio, Axl Rose sings about walking in the cold autumn rain. The wipers sweep across the windshield. He turns up the song and follows his headlights through the darkness.

~*~

Robby takes a shopping cart from the far side of the parking lot and jams it into the line of carts that he's already accumulated. Wiping his palm across his brow, he looks at it and then dries it down the front of his shirt. Pushing his knuckles into his lower back, he stretches. Across the lot, a woman closes the back hatch on her minivan. She gives her cart a shove toward the cart corral some twenty-five feet away. Sliding in behind her steering wheel, she closes the door and drives off. Her cart rolls listlessly toward the corral before slowly veering off into a driving lane. It rattles across the asphalt and comes to a banging stop against the front bumper of someone else's car.

Robby shakes his head and laughs disgustedly. At the distant entrance of the store, the customers are like hornets in and out of a hive. He watches them and exhales an exhausted breath. Leaning his weight into the line of shopping carts nested together in front of him, he glances to his left and watches a truck pull out of a far corner parking spot. The truck's departure reveals a shopping cart sitting in the farthest possible corner of the lot.

Robby stands up straight and stares at it. He flips his damp hair from his eyes. "You're fucking kidding me." He points at it. "You little bitch. Hiding from me, huh?" After a moment, he jogs halfheartedly toward it.

~*~

A dark gray Cadillac pulls into the adjacent parking spot as

Robby grabs the cart's handle. The driver's side window slides down.

Robby turns. His face pales.

"Get in the car," the driver says, nostrils flaring.

Mouth hanging open, Robby stares at the driver's grim face, his bald head. The man's jaw looks as though it could take a kick from a horse. Robby takes a step back.

"Get in the fucking car. Don't even think about running."

Robby stammers. "I was going to come see—"

"Shut the fuck up and get in the car."

He nods. "Okay. Okay," he says, walking around to the passenger side door. He opens it, slides in, and closes it again.

He turns toward the man. "Really, I was going to—"

The man clamps his vice-grip hand around Robby's neck and pins his head against the passenger window. "Turn your pockets inside out."

"Andre…"

"Now!"

With his face flattened against the glass, Robby grunts a breath and wriggles his fingers down into his pockets. He pulls out the insides. Some coins fall down into the footwell. An old receipt drifts down onto the seat.

"Now lift up your shirt."

"I don't have anything—"

Andre jerks his head back a few inches and then slams it against the glass again. "Lift up your fucking shirt. All the way around."

"Okay. Okay." He pulls up the shirt, exposing his mid-section.

Andre looks at his waistband and then leans him forward, pressing his face into the dashboard. After a moment, he releases his neck.

Robby pulls his shirt down and tucks his pockets back in. He sweeps his bangs aside. His breaths are arrhythmic. "I was going to come see you. I just wanted to have something—"

"Shut the fuck up."

Robby rubs his hand over his face. He breathes in a strained breath through his nose.

Andre sits turned toward him. His left hand rests on the steering wheel, his grip squeezing and then letting go. He is wearing black jeans and a striped, button up short sleeve shirt, untucked. Veins snake along his forearms. He shakes his head. "A month you been out a that place. A fucking month...and you don't come see me? What...did you think I'd forget?"

Robby exhales into his palm. "I wanted to have something, Andre. I wanted to have a chunk with me to give you—"

Andre crosses his arms. "You borrowed three thousand dollars from me. Three fucking thousand."

He nods quickly. "I know. I know—"

"You never made one payment. Not one fucking payment in eight months."

He holds his hands prayer-like against his lips. He close his eyes. "I know. I'm sorry. I know. I was—"

Across the parking lot, a little boy bolts from a car. The mother takes three long strides and catches him by the arm. He cries and pulls against her grip.

Andre pinches the end of his nose and then looks at his thumb and finger tips. "So now, it's six thousand you owe me. All right?"

Robby opens his eyes wide. "Six thousand? That's—"

"That's a fucking bargain," Andre says, pointing. "I could be holding your ass to a lot more than that. That three thousand is money I couldn't loan to anyone else for eight months. Eight fucking months."

Robby stares out the windshield. Cars pull in and out of the parking spots. People stream in and out of the store. They put groceries in their trunks. In the distance, the parking lot hazes with the heat rising from the asphalt.

"I want half of it in two weeks. The principal. No more fucking around, all right?"

He looks at him. "Two weeks? I don't think I can—"

Andre locks his eyes on his and points his finger in his face. "Find a way. Sell your mom's car. Steal something and don't get caught like a little bitch this time. I don't care how you do it, but I want that fucking money in two weeks."

Robby looks out the windshield again. He stares, slack-jawed.

After a moment, Andre snorts a mean laugh. "Yeah, you sit and turn that shit over in your head. Be a dumbass."

"What?"

"Running. That's what you're thinking. 'Shit, I could just bail. Just take off. It's not like he'd come after me if I—'"

He shakes his head, his eyes pleading with Andre's. "I wasn't thinking that."

"You don't think I could find your sorry little ass?"

"Andre, I wasn't thinking—"

He snaps his thick fingers. "Within a week…tops." He looks at Robby and shakes his head. "Piss-ant like you…probably three days."

"I—"

"Then it'd get ugly. Fucking ugly."

Robby drops his face into his hands. "Andre—"

"What the fuck you doing borrowing money from me, anyway? You got in over your head in a big fucking hurry. Little suburb boy. Got a shit mouth full of lies."

Face still in his hands, he nods. "I know."

"Selling me a line about lawn mowing equipment that you could get cheap. A rider, weed whacker, edger…the whole deal, you said."

Robby squeezes his hands on the top of his head. "I know. I—"

"Said you didn't know if it was stolen or what, but you were going to start your own business with it. Said you'd have me paid back in no time. But you needed the money in a hurry. The whole deal was on a timer, you said."

Silent, Robby holds his head.

"They should give out awards for being able to tell lies like that." Andre is quiet a moment. "Smart though, too. If I'd known the truth, I wouldn't have borrowed you shit. Fucking useless addict."

"I wasn't thinking straight," he whispers.

"You snort up the Cotton you're supposed to be selling for your dealer…and then you come to me for the money out of it?"

He nods.

"You weren't scared of that pharmy, were you? Scared of what he'd do if he didn't get his money back?"

"No. I was just trying to get away from him…be done with him.

I wanted to try to get—"

"Shut the fuck up. Don't interrupt me." Andre shakes his head. "Out of the two of us, I'm the one you should have been afraid of."

Robby lifts his head and brushes his cheeks with his fingertips. With the fingers of both hands, he combs his hair back over the top of his head. His attention snaps to across the parking lot where a man in a tie stands with his hands on his hips. "That's my boss."

Andre looks. "I don't give a shit."

He puts his fingers and thumb on the door handle. "Two weeks. I'll have your money in two weeks."

Andre looks across the lot at Robby's manager walking toward the car. "You ain't gonna get three grand working this shithole. Not in two weeks. Not with all the overtime in the world."

"I know. I'll think of something." He lifts the door handle.

Andre's fingers and thumb clamp down over Robby's other wrist and hold him in place. "Aren't you scared I might kill you, Robby?"

Wide-eyed, he stares at Andre's hand.

He snorts a laugh. "Don't piss yourself. What the hell would that get me? Nothing. A dead body, and I'd still be out my money."

Robby looks into his face. He blinks.

"See, I'm not going to hurt you. Never had any payoff from hurting my clients." He smiles and nods. "I will hurt people that mean something to you , though. If I have to…if that's what you push me to."

Robby shakes his head. "You won't have to—"

"You run, and your mom will be the one in pain. Or that girl you knocked up."

"I'm not going to run."

Andre nods. "Good." He tightens his grip. "You understand me though, right?" He squeezes harder.

Robby winces, nodding.

"Did your girl tell you about the flower one of my boys left for her…right on her counter?" He smiles. "Yeah, she told you. I can see it in your face." He releases his wrist. "That was just a little something to let you know how easily I can get to people…especially if you run."

Robby's face is pale. "I'm not going to."

"Good boy."

He rubs his wrist. "Christ."

"Robby?"

He turns. Andre punches him in the cheek, bouncing the other side of his skull off the passenger side window. As Robby holds his head, Andre reaches across his lap, opens the door, and pushes him out onto the asphalt.

"Two weeks," he says, pulling the door closed and then starting the engine. He drives off.

~*~

Sitting on the asphalt, Robby rubs his cheek, opening and closing his jaw.

"I don't want to know. Don't even try to explain it to me."

He looks between his fingers at his manager standing some ten feet away. "I won't."

"Good. When you can, go inside and punch out. I'll have payroll cut your final check. You can pick it up at the service desk."

"Okay. Thanks, Clark."

Clark studies him a moment before shaking his head and walking away. Coming to it, he leans into the line of carts Robby had gathered and pushes it rattling toward the store.

Robby rubs his cheek and watches him disappear.

~*~

Otto lifts the garage door, sending it rolling along its tracks into the ceiling. Resting his palms against the door's weatherstripping, he leans and stretches his upper back. "There she is, boy," he moans, still stretching his muscles.

Robby looks inside the garage. Next to his grandfather's Taurus is the outline of another car concealed under a fitted cover.

"That's the Bird," Otto says.

"It's been a long time since I've seen it," Robby says. "Dad showed it to me once when I was a kid."

"Never had it out much." Otto clenches and unclenches his fingers, taking a few steps toward the passenger's side of the cover. "Get that other side," he says.

They bend down to the bumper and peel back the dust cover, revealing first the side-by-side headlights and then the heart-red front end of a '68 Pontiac Firebird.

Robby whistles, still folding the cloth back.

"Whoa, slow down," Otto says. He shimmies the cover up and over the radio antennae. "Okay, now we can take it the rest of the way back."

Once they're finished, Robby stands admiring the car. Otto folds the billowy cover against his chest. The red body shines brilliantly in the sunlight coming through the garage window.

"That's good ol' fashion Detroit muscle there, boy."

Robby paces back and forth in front of the headlights surveying the car. "What's a car like this worth, Grandpa?"

Otto gestures his chin toward the Firebird. "Don't let that paint job fool you. She ain't perfect. Far from mint and lots of miles. I probably babied her more than she deserved." He walks toward the work bench. "About ten years back, I had a guy tell me that she's worth maybe eight. In this economy, who knows."

Robby kneels down and looks at himself in the paint of the driver's side fender. "Badass set of wheels."

"Well, it's no chickenshit Prius, that's for sure." He sets the cover down on the work bench. "You think you'll be able to handle it?"

He stands, nodding his head. "Oh, yeah." He snaps his neck, and his hair flips from his eyes.

"Still can't locate a barber, can ya?" Otto walks over to the driver's side. Taking keys from his pocket, he unlocks the door, opens it, and slides into the seat. Leaving the door open, he grips the wheel in both hands and leans back into the vinyl. His eyes go far away as he stares out the windshield. "Your old man helped me with a lot of the restoration on this car."

Robby nods. "I remember him saying that."

He puts the key in the ignition. "Spent almost two years out here together. Lions on the radio in the fall, Red Wings in the winter, and the Tigers all spring and summer. That was a good two years." He nods to himself. "He worked his ass off on this car. Never a complaint out of him." He slides a finger along the steering wheel and whispers sympathetically. "Course the other boys…"

Robby looks at him. "What?"

He glares back at him. "So how the hell much am I paying you to take this little road trip with me?"

Robby swallows. "Like I said on the phone, I was thinking like a thousand bucks. You said that you were okay with it."

"I know. I just wanted to hear it again to make sure I was hearing it right." He scratches his fingers into his white hair. "Jesus Christ, time with your grandson is expensive anymore."

Robby leans against the fender of the Taurus. "It's a week. It's less than six bucks an hour if you look at it that way."

Otto crosses his arms. "But you'll be paying for your own meals at least, right?"

He looks at the floor.

Otto shakes his head. "Holy cow. This whole thing might not even be worth it."

He bolts up off the Taurus. "Grandpa, I quit my job at the grocery store to do this."

"Well, who the hell told you to do that?"

He stuffs his hands in his pockets. "Nobody. It's just that the last time I was here, you made it sound like this was something you really wanted to do. You made it—"

"Well, maybe it is, but I don't want to go broke doing it. What the hell do you need that much money for, anyway?"

Robby stares blank-eyed at his grandfather's face. Then, scratching behind his ear, he nods. "School," he says. "I want to register for the fall. I want to have enough saved up so maybe I can just concentrate on my classes and not have to worry about working."

Otto studies him. "School," he says. "Well, it sure as hell doesn't make sense you quitting your job if you're saving up for school."

Robby crosses his arms. "There's not a lot of places that give you a week's vacation after only working three weeks. It's about the only way I could make the trip with you."

Nodding almost imperceptibly, Otto sits a moment. Then, he

pulls the door closed on the Firebird and looks out the window at Robby. "You want to hear the engine?"

Robby leans against the Taurus again. "Fire it up."

The Firebird's combusting thunders into the space of the garage. Its idling growls its potential kinetic energy. Otto presses the gas pedal a few times, revving the engine. A thin film of exhaust hangs in the air. Smiling, Robby covers his ears.

"You like that?" Otto shouts.

He laughs, nodding.

He cuts the engine. "That's what a car is supposed to sound like, boy. You're too used to these wind-up toys everyone drives now." He pats his hand on the dashboard. "In my day, if a car didn't rattle your balls numb, it wasn't a car."

"Well, we sure aren't going to be sneaking up on anyone."

Otto opens the door and uses the window frame to pull himself up. "That we won't." Standing, he smiles at him. "Wouldn't be a bad idea if we could."

"What?"

"Nothing."

Robby crosses his arms. "You still thinking of leaving tomorrow?"

Otto walks toward the sunlight outside of the garage. A car drives past on the street. "Tomorrow's Sunday. Be a good day for driving north. Everyone else will be heading south." Looking out at the neighborhood, he stands with his hands on his hips. "I want to go to Uncle Paulie's first."

He studies his grandfather's back. "Why would we go to Traverse City first? Isn't Uncle Jack just up in Flint?"

Otto turns around and waves him out of the garage. "Don't worry about it. It's already all planned out. Just get out of there now and let me close this up."

Robby walks out into the sunlight. A sprinkler arcs back and forth on the neighbor's front lawn. He watches it. The wet grass blades glimmer in the sunlight.

"You're clean right?" Otto asks, crossing his arms.

"What? Yeah, I'm still… Grandpa? What are you—"

"It's nothing. It's just that a guy can fall off the wagon, that's all."

He walks over and reaches up for the handle of the garage door. "I can't have you driving that car if you're... If you're still using, we can't do this."

Robby swallows. "I'm not using."

"That's all I wanted to know." He pulls the garage door down slowly. "I'll see you tomorrow then."

"Grandpa..."

Otto waves a hand at him. "Just have your mom drop you off here tomorrow by nine."

"Okay."

Robby looks back and catches one more glimpse of the Firebird's frontend. Biting his thumbnail, he walks across the front lawn to his mother's car parked at the curb.

Robby opens the door to Shuette's car dealership. Parked at angles, a Ford Fusion, Flex, and Mustang gleam on the showroom floor. Flipping his hair from his face, he looks around at the glass-walled offices. A few of the men in the cubicles look his way, study him a moment, and then look back to their computer screens or the papers on their desks. After a moment, one of the men hangs up a phone. He looks Robby over and then pushes himself up with the arms of his chair. He walks out of his office to where Robby is looking at one of the cars.

The salesman wears a suit, a mustache, and his thinning hair is slicked back over his head. He smiles with overly-white teeth. "Mustang man, eh? We can talk deal if you're looking to drive this out of here today."

He looks at him and shakes his head. "I'm not looking for a car. I'm looking for Tiffany."

"Who?"

"Tiffany. Tiffany Whiting. She's a receptionist here."

The man's face sours. He points. "The reception desk is over there." He walks back toward his office. One of the guys in another office points at the salesman and laughs. The salesman gives him the finger.

Robby walks to the reception desk and finds Tiffany on the phone.

"I can transfer you to him," she says. She looks up and sees Robby. Her brows furrow. "Okay. Here you go. Have a good day." She hangs up the phone. "Robby, what are you doing here?"

He shrugs. "I just wanted to talk."

She looks around. "You shouldn't be here."

"I just wanted to see you before I go." He crosses his arms and shrugs. "I'm going on a road trip."

Her hands go to her belly. "A road trip? What road trip?"

~*~

Behind the dealership, Tiffany sits in one of the two lawn chairs in the shade of the building. There's a coffee can full of sand and cigarette butts near the door. Robby crouches down on one knee and leans his back against the aluminum siding. The sounds of the mechanics working on cars whines from the open service bay doors.

"That's really nice," Tiffany says, "what you're doing for your grandpa."

He shrugs a shoulder. "It's no big deal."

"They gave you the time off from work?"

He shakes his head. "No, I had to quit. It doesn't matter, though. That job was going nowhere. I'll look for something else when we get back."

Her hands work their circles. "You said about a week?"

"Week, maybe a couple days more."

She looks at her hands. "I was going to ask you to help me, but I don't think you'll be here now."

He looks at her profile. "Help you?"

"I'm moving. I just had a few things that I could use a hand with."

He leans off the wall and switches knees. "Where are you moving?"

She doesn't turn his way. Her gaze is distant and unfocused. "Back in with my mom."

A younger guy drives around the side of the building and parks a Ford Focus in one of the empty parking spaces. He cuts the engine and runs inside the service doors.

Robby clears his throat. "Living with your mom…that will be a big help when the baby comes."

She nods, looking at her hands again. "That's what she says."

"You'll save a lot of money, too."

She smiles, nodding. Then, she turns and looks at him. Her smile is gone. "It all sounds good, but I don't want to move back home. I really don't." She touches her fingertips over her lips. "I really wanted to do this on my own, you know?"

He stands up, wincing as his knees unbend. "Why are you doing it?"

She looks away toward the houses on the other side of the street across from the dealership. "It doesn't feel like I have a choice. Dan's hiring someone else for the title clerk position."

"What? Why?"

She shrugs. "A guy with five years of experience applied last week. Dan told me that he didn't have a choice." She looks at her stilled hands. "He said that if something opens up down the road, it's mine."

He crosses his arms. "That's not right. He promised you that position."

"Right has nothing to do with it. He needs someone now."

"It still sucks."

Her hands start moving again. "At least moving back home will get me out of that apartment. I've been freaked out living there ever since that break-in."

Robby closes his eyes and squeezes a hand into a fist. He opens his eyes again. "Did the police ever find out anything?"

"No. They didn't know what to make of it. They were asking me questions about old boyfriends."

Robby laces his fingers together and cracks his knuckles. "Did you tell them about Mikey?"

She shakes her head. "I don't think he'd do that."

"Probably not."

"The last thing he needs is the police coming around asking him questions," she says, shaking her head.

"That's probably true."

A man wearing a dress shirt and tie comes out of the backdoor of the dealership. His salt and pepper hair is parted to the side.

"Hey, Todd," Tiffany says.

He cups his hand around the top of a lighter and flicks a flame up to the cigarette in his mouth. "Hey." He takes a drag and exhales. "Slow as shit in there today."

"Yeah."

He takes a few more puffs and then looks at Robby. "You in the market for a car?"

Robby shakes his head.

Todd takes another drag and looks at Tiffany, at her belly. Then he looks back at Robby. Smiling, he walks off toward the doors of the service garage. "I'm sure I'll see you later."

"Okay," she says.

Robby takes a few steps away from the building. "You know, you wouldn't have to stay at your mom's for long. When I get back and get another job, I could help you pay rent on an apartment."

"Robby—"

"I mean, I'm living for free at my mom's place, so I'd have extra money. She said that I can stay as long as I need to."

She's quiet for a moment behind him. "I couldn't let you do that."

He shoves his hands into his pockets. "It's not like it'd be charity or anything." He shrugs. "I mean, I should be helping to—"

"I should get back inside."

He turns around. Standing slowly, Tiffany follows her belly up out of the chair.

He inhales a breath that catches staccato along his throat. "Is this the way it's always going to be?"

She looks at him. "What do you mean?"

His hands flip in the air in front of him. "I don't know, it's just…I love you. I always have—"

"Robby, don't."

He takes a step toward her. "Why not? I'm just telling you how I feel. I'm sick of keeping it to myself."

"Robby—"

"You're saying that you don't feel anything for me?"

She looks at the ground. "My break is over."

"I don't care."

"Robby..."

"I mean, why did you sleep with me that night after I told you I loved you?" He waits a second. "And don't even start talking about how drunk you were because you weren't even drunk. That's not even fair to say."

She rubs her hands up and down her arms. "No, I really wasn't drunk."

"Well, then—"

"I just don't think that we would be good for each other. Everything is different now." She looks at the ground again. "I need to grow up, and you have too much that you need to figure out."

He crosses his arms. "I don't need to figure out how I feel about you."

Tiffany looks toward the service garage. Robby follows her gaze. Todd walks toward them, lighting another cigarette.

"I have to go," she says.

He sweeps his fingers through his hair, pushing his bangs from his face. "You don't have any feelings for me then?"

She turns away.

"Tif?"

She opens the door.

"Tif...I'm going to call you from the road, okay?"

She starts to walk inside.

"Okay?"

She pauses a moment and then disappears into the darkness beyond the doorway. The door closes. He stands staring at it.

Todd walks up and stands with his foot near the coffee can of cigarette butts. "I got nothing but time if you want to take something out for a road test."

Robby looks at him. "What?" He shakes his head. "No."

Todd smiles and bends to flick an ash into the can. "Can't blame a guy for trying, right?"

Robby starts to walk away.

"If you change your mind, ask for Todd Walker. I'll get you a good deal."

Robby waves his hand in the air over the back of his head. He walks around the side of the dealership and back to the front. Weaving through the cars, he gets to his mother's car. He looks at the dealership's windows. A half-acre of cars is reflected there. His own reflection— chest, neck, and head—is among them. He looks at himself and then flips his overgrown bang from his face.

His cell phone vibrates.

"Goddamnit," he says, fishing it from his pocket. He looks at the screen.

A text from Tif: *Call from the road if u want*

He smiles.

~*~

Otto opens the door to Robby standing on his stoop. He smiles. "Well, look at Mr. Haircut. I'd forgot that you had green eyes."

Robby waves his fingers through his hair. "Mom butchered me. I look like I'm ready for boot camp."

Otto reaches down into one of his pockets. "Not quite boot camp regulation, boy, but you look a helluva lot better than you did." He pulls out a set of keys and hands them to him. "Put your stuff in the trunk and then fire up the Bird. I'll be out in a minute." He shuffles back into the house.

Robby looks over his shoulder at the Firebird shining in the driveway. He smiles, tosses the keys up in the air, and then catches them.

~*~

Just after 23 merges with 75, a GM plant stretches out in parking lots and buildings on the east side of the highway.

Otto sits up and looks out his window. "Look at all that parking," he says. "For who?"

Robby glances. "It's Sunday, Grandpa."

Otto looks over at him. "Drive by here any day of the week,

you'll see the same. It's like a ghost town."

Robby looks over at the building's wall of windows.

"Just keep your eyes on the road, boy. Nothing to see over there."

~*~

They drive north of Mt. Morris on I-75. Trees and scrub-field flank either side of the highway for miles. Otto sleeps with his head against the passenger side window. Robby stares out the windshield past the hood tachometer. The Firebird's engine growls.

He squeezes the steering wheel and shakes his head. Then, he turns on the radio. Turning the knob through the stations, he finds 103.9, The Fox, a classic rock station out of Flint. The Who's "Who are You?" plays.

Otto stirs. Robby reaches for the knob and turns down the volume.

He plays the steering wheel like a bass string. Roger Daltrey howls out the question.

"Turn that off," Otto says, eyes still closed.

Robby reaches and turns the song down more.

"Off, I said."

He looks at him and then back at the road. "Aren't you sleeping?"

"Not with that on, I'm not."

Robby turns the radio off. He looks at the endless trees around them and the endless trees continuing into the distance. He shakes his head.

Otto passes gas.

~*~

Robby drives slowly down Carroll Road on Old Mission Peninsula. Mammoth houses rise up from the various shades of green all around them. Rows and rows of cherry trees order the landscape on either side of the road. A blue sky backgrounds it all.

"This is money, boy."

Robby glances around.

"Right here," Otto says, pointing.

He pulls the Firebird into a long driveway and then right behind a silver Lexus. Wearing a polo shirt and khakis, his Uncle Paul stands at the driver's side of the car looking as though he's about to get in. He squints over his shoulder at the Pontiac. His left hand drifts up and covers his mouth as he stares at the car. His head shakes back and forth slowly. His eyes are cold.

Beyond him looms a beautiful two-story home sided in cedar shakes. The front lawn stretches with grass immaculate enough to be in a commercial. Small islands of mulch and decorative stone feature weeping mulberries, Crabapple Tina, Cleveland Pear and other ornamental trees.

Otto opens his door and uses it to pull himself to standing. "Hey there, Paulie. You look like you're seeing a ghost."

Paul's mouth says something and he points at Robby.

Robby rolls down his window.

"That's just Robby," Otto says, "Gerry's boy." He leans down and looks at Robby in the driver's seat. "Don't just sit there like a lump, boy. Get out and say hi."

He gets out of the car and stands behind his open door. "Hi, Uncle Paul."

Paul lifts his hand and waves. "Robby, how are you?"

"Not bad."

Paul smiles and then looks back at Otto. He scratches his head. "What are you doing here, Dad?"

Otto points at the house. "Quite a place you got here, Paulie. Regular Taj Mahal."

The passenger door on the Lexus opens. Robby's Aunt Stephanie stands up out of the car and shifts her sunglasses from her eyes up to the top of her head. Her blonde hair is shoulder-length, and she wears a floral summer dress. Her arms and legs are thin. A visible vein runs down each taut bicep. "Hello, Otto." She smiles.

"Good to see you, Stephanie. I was just telling Paulie that you have a beautiful home."

"Just Paul, Dad."

"Thank you," Stepahnie says. She looks. "Hi, Robby."

Robby waves his hand. "Hi." He musses his fingers through his short hair. "Good to see you, Aunt Stephanie."

"You too. It's been awhile." She looks across the car at Paul.

He stretches his arm out and sets his palm flat on the roof, shrugging his shoulder toward his ear. "So, what are you doing here, Dad?"

Otto closes his door and then crosses his arms. "Just wanted to come see you, I guess. That's okay, isn't it?"

Paul pushes his fingers through his hair, pressing it in place. "It's fine." He clears his throat. "It's just that today isn't really good. We're on our way to see friends in Petoskey."

"Paul," Stephanie says.

He looks at her. "What? We are."

Otto shuffles a couple steps forward. "It's just been a long time."

"That's true," Paul says, nodding. He scratches his cheek. "Where are you two staying?"

Otto smiles. "Nowhere yet. We just got into town and we drove straight here. Don't worry. We'll take a hotel."

Robby looks at his grandfather and then at his grim-faced uncle.

Paul nods. "We're going to be up in Petoskey for a couple days," he says. "The timing's not really good."

Stephanie looks as though she's going to say something but then doesn't.

Otto leans against the Firebird's fender. "Five-hour drive up here." He looks over at Robby. "We stopped in West Branch for lunch. Stopped a couple times for gas too. Doubt this beast even gets fifteen miles to the gallon. Other than that, we were on the road."

"Well, you should have…" Paul crosses his arms and then holds a long shrug. "I mean, the timing's just really bad. We've had these plans for a couple weeks."

"Paul…" Stephanie starts.

He checks her with a look and then looks back at Otto. "Maybe I could come down to your place after we get back." He glances at the ground and then up again. "Work's been really crazy, but I might be able to make it down for a day. I couldn't stay over or anything, but I could visit for a while."

"I would have called, Paulie, but you never—"

Paul holds up his palm. "I'll get in touch with you when we get back, Dad. Okay? We'll try to work something out. I promise."

Otto's gaze drops down to the trunk of the Lexus. He nods. "Okay, Paulie. We'll see what we can work out. Like you said, just bad timing, I guess."

He nods. "Yeah."

Otto doesn't move. He rubs his hand absently on the hood of the Firebird. A robin lands in the branches of one of the mulberry trees.

"Otto," Stephanie says.

Both Paul and Otto look at her.

"Why don't you come in for a bit? I mean, it's crazy for you..." She looks at Paul's stunned face and then quickly looks back at Otto. "I can call our friends and tell them that we'll be a couple hours late. She'll understand."

Paul takes a long breath and exhales.

"Well, I wouldn't mind at least using your restroom," Otto says. "My plumbing doesn't work like it used to."

Paul sniffs a mean laugh and shakes his head.

Stephanie closes her door. "Of course. I can fix you a snack, too. You must be a little hungry if you haven't eaten since West Branch."

"Fix yourself a snack, too," Otto says, smiling. "You're wasting away."

Paul shoves his door closed. Rubbing his fingers across his chin, he glares at the sky.

"We can give you a little tour of the place," Stephanie says, turning toward the house. She doesn't look at her husband.

Otto starts walking after her. "I'd like that. I've never seen it." He doesn't look toward Paul, but follows his daughter-in-law.

Paul looks over his shoulder at Stephanie and Otto going up the driveway. "I'll be right there," he calls.

Robby closes his door.

Paul looks his way, studies him a moment, and then motions his chin toward the Firebird. "How did it drive?"

"Good. No problems."

Paul walks down to the front of the car and leans his palms down on the hood. "Gerry and Otto's baby. Their special little project."

"What?"

Paul glances at him. "Nothing."

Robby looks at the house. "You really have a great place, Uncle Paul."

He stands up straight and crosses his arms. His silver Rolex catches the sun. "So what's he doing up here?"

"He didn't really say."

"He didn't say," Paul repeats.

Robby shakes his head.

"Why are you with him?"

He picks a thumbnail against the other. "He needed somebody to drive him. He said he's not supposed to be driving."

"Why?"

"Didn't say."

Paul looks at him. "Man of mystery, eh?"

Robby smiles and shrugs. "I guess so." He shifts his weight to his other foot. "How's Tyler?"

"Really good. He's doing PR work in Chicago."

Robby nods.

"Public relations," Paul says.

Robby nods again.

Paul looks at him until Robby averts his eyes.

"Look," Paul says, "if you know why he's here, just tell me. What do I need to brace myself for?"

Robby shrugs his hands into the air. "I really don't know. He just said that it's been a long time and he wanted to see you and Uncle Jack."

Paul exhales a laugh. "Uncle Jack? How did that go?"

"We haven't seen him yet."

He studies Robby. "Your Uncle Jack is in Flint."

"I know."

Otto's voice comes from the side yard of the house saying something to Stephanie.

Paul looks over his shoulder toward his house and then back at Robby. "Let me guess, he didn't say why he wanted to come see me before seeing Jack."

"Not to me he didn't."

Paul shakes his head and then stands up straight, saying nothing. Then, "Well, we might as well go in and get this over with." He starts walking toward the house.

After a moment, Robby follows him.

~*~

They sit on Paul's second story deck. It overlooks one of the wine vineyards that stretches green to the horizon and ends at a blue wall of lake and sky.

Otto holds a glass of lemonade. "That work?" he asks, pointing to a fireplace on the deck.

"Yes," Stephanie says, "It's gas. It's beautiful at night."

"I don't think I've ever seen one outside before."

Paul's glass of lemonade sits sweating in front of him on the table. He's leaned into his chair with his arms crossed. He glances at his watch.

Robby drinks the last of his lemonade. The ice cubes hit his lips.

Otto makes himself another cracker. "Goat cheese, huh? Tastes a lot better than I would have guessed. Not something I'd ever buy."

Stephanie smiles. "When I first tried it—?"

"So, are you two getting back on the road tonight?" Paul asks. "To a hotel or whatever."

Stephanie snaps a look at her husband.

Otto chews and then swallows. "Not sure what the plan is. Getting a little late for driving."

"Sunday night. Should be able to get a hotel room in town," Paul says. He picks up his glass, tilts it back and forth in his grip, and then sets it down again. "It'll be expensive, though. Nothing cheap in TC."

Otto looks at him. "I'm not too worried about it."

"That's a change," Paul says. "You never used to be one for spending money on nice hotels. Or on anything."

Stephanie adjusts herself in her seat.

"No, I suppose I wasn't."

Paul looks at Stephanie. "Did I ever tell you about the summer Dad took us to Tawas for a beach vacation?" He looks at Otto. "Tawas, right?"

Looking sheepish, he nods.

"That was some trip." Paul turns to Stephanie again. "We stayed in this flea bag place outside of town. God, what a dump. It had to have been a fifteen-minute drive from the beach." He looks at Otto again. "What was the name of that place?"

Otto sets the other half of his cracker down on his plate and stares at it. "I don't really remember."

"Paul..." Stephanie starts.

"Jack and I were so excited. Dad was going to rent a fishing boat. That was the big plan. That's why he said he wanted to save money on the motel, so we could get the best boat the marina had. We were going to catch some lake trout, right Dad?" He laughs and shakes his head. "Remember, though? You were so hung over the morning we were supposed to go that we never—"

"I think I'll go in and double check that I packed everything," Stephanie says, standing up. "I always forget something." She touches Paul's shoulder until he looks at her. Her look communicates something to him.

His face changes, softens. After a moment with her fingers on his shoulder, she pulls back a sliding glass door and disappears inside.

Otto scoots the cracker forward with his fingertip. "That trip was a long time ago, Paulie."

"Paul, Dad. Just Paul, okay?"

"Okay. Sorry."

"And, a lot of things happened a long time ago."

"That's true," Otto says.

"That doesn't erase them."

Robby sets his hands in his lap and looks at them. He softly bites his lower lip.

Picking up his lemonade as though to take a drink, Paul holds it in front of his face. He studies it, turning it back and forth. Then, he looks at Otto. "Dad, you got me curious as hell here. What did you have Robby drive you all the way up here for?"

Otto pulls his lemonade glass close to the edge of the table and holds it there. "Do you hear much from Jack?"

"No. I haven't talked to him since Gerry's..." He glances at Robby. "I haven't talked to him."

Robby watches his own fingers scratching his wrist. He sniffs a breath through his nose.

"You guys don't keep in touch?"

"No, we don't." Paul bangs his glass back down on the table. "Dad, we have this thing up in Petoskey? Can you tell me why you're here?"

Otto squeezes his hand into a fist and winces. "Ooh. Damn arthritis is getting worse every day."

"Dad."

"Okay. Okay." He stands up and walks to the railing of the deck. He rubs his leg. "Robby and me are on a little road trip. It's going to end this Friday with us up in Grand Marais...at Grandpa's old cabin up there."

"Okay," Paul says.

"Well, I'd like it if you drove up there and met us Saturday morning."

"What?"

Otto turns around and faces the table. "Now, I only say Saturday for you because that will give me and Robby a chance to get the place ready."

Paul massages his forehead. "Ready for what?"

"A guy's weekend. I'm going to invite your brother, too." He takes a step forward. "We can grill some steaks, my treat. Hell, we could probably even charter a boat out of Grand Marais. Make up for—"

"Dad—"

Otto holds up his hand. "Now just hear me out. I want to spend a little time with you boys. I want to give you a nice weekend—"

Paul laughs. "A nice weekend in Grandpa's shack? That place probably isn't even standing anymore."

"No, it's fine. I got a guy that looks in on it for me. And you said that you were going to drive down to my place, so just drive up there instead."

Paul shakes his head. "Why, Dad? Why? Why in God's name would we go up to Grand Marais? Why would I want to spend a weekend with you and Jack up there? Why would I—"

Otto slaps his hand on the railing of the deck and points at him. "Because, goddamnit, I want to spend a little time with you and your brother. Is that so goddamn hard to understand?"

Wide-eyed, Robby looks at his grandfather.

After a moment, Paul smiles wryly. He picks up his lemonade glass and toasts it toward his father. "And there he is, folks. The Otto Cooper we all know is finally here. Where you been hiding?"

He puts his hand to his forehead. "Look, I'm sorry. I didn't mean to snap…I just want to spend a little time with you and your brother. I want to talk—"

"About what? What do you want to talk about? You drove all the way up here. Why can't you just say what you have to say right now?"

Otto looks at the floor and hitches up his pants. "Because I'm not ready right now. And what I want to say, I want to say to both of you together."

Paul shakes his head. "It's an apology, isn't it? You want—"

"Paulie… Paul. Don't answer right now, okay? I'm—"

"Do you have any idea what my memories of going up to Grandpa's place with you are like? Do you have any idea what any of my memories are like?"

Otto nods. "I know. But it's not going to be like that. You know I quit…years ago, I quit. This time—"

"It's going to be great, boys," Paul says, mimicking Otto's voice. "This time's going to be different. This time we're going to have a great time and—"

"Don't be an ass, Paulie."

Stephanie slides open the door. She looks at the two of them glaring at each other. She makes a smile and raises her eyebrows. "Does anybody need anything out here?"

A moment passes.

"No, we're good," Paul says, still looking at Otto. "We're just finishing up. I'll be in in a minute. Then we can go."

"Okay." She looks at them again and then slides the door closed.

Otto takes a long breath and then exhales. "This is important to me. That might not mean shit to you, and I guess I really don't blame you. I'm just here to tell you that me and Robby will be up there. I really want you to come up—" He holds up his hand. "Don't say anything right now, okay? Just come up there. I'm saying that I want my sons to come up there and be with me…just for this weekend. After that, well then whatever you like."

"Dad—"

"I'm getting older, Paulie."

Paul shakes his head. "Jesus Christ."

Otto waits a moment. "We're going now. Okay?" He looks at Robby. "Get up, boy. Let's go."

Robby nods and stands.

"Dad—"

Otto stops and looks at the floor. "You're my son. Both you boys, you're my sons. Okay?" He looks at Paul. "Nothing changes that. I know I don't have the right to ask anything of you, but I'm asking you this. I'm asking."

Paul stares at the distant horizon, shaking his head. "Unbelievable."

"We'll take the stairs." Otto shuffles toward the flight of stairs that will take them down to the backyard. "Any time on Saturday, okay? But try for around noon. Tell Stephanie that we said goodbye."

Paul doesn't move, doesn't say anything.

Otto holds the railing and starts slowly down. He watches his feet.

Stepping down the first step, Robby looks back. "See ya, Uncle Paul."

Seemingly oblivious, Paul glares into the distance, saying nothing.

~*~

Robby and Otto stand by the open trunk of the Firebird in the parking lot of the Park Place Hotel in downtown Traverse City. Otto gazes up the side of the building washed in the light of the sun. Robby takes his phone out of his pocket, checks the time, and then slides it back in.

"Your grandmother and I used to come up here every year for the Cherry Festival," Otto says. "For about fifteen years in a row, we did."

Robby nods. "I remember. You took me once."

"You complained the whole time, too."

"Yeah," he says. "Probably." He reaches into the trunk and takes out his duffel bag, setting it on the ground.

Otto looks up the height of the hotel again. "Your grandmother always wanted to stay here. She talked about how great it would be to be right downtown where we could walk to everything if we wanted. There's a lounge up on the top floor." He pinches his nose between his thumb and fingers. "She always wondered what the view would be like from up there. It was kind of a bucket list thing for her."

Robby lifts Otto's bag out. He closes the trunk and looks up at the hotel. "Looks like a nice place."

Otto shifts his back, lifting one shoulder and then the other. He moans. "I fought her tooth and nail every time. 'Too damn expensive', I said. We always ended up staying in some motel five or six miles outside of town."

Robby picks up his bag.

Otto looks at him. "Don't be like that if you can help it," he says. "Being a tightwad, it's no good."

He shrugs and then nods. They start walking toward the lobby entrance. A couple walks out laughing and holding hands.

"So, what do you think, boy…want something to eat? They got a restaurant right in the hotel."

"Actually," he says, "if you don't mind, I think I'll take a walk around downtown. I'm not really hungry right now."

"That's fine. I'm a little filled up on goat cheese and crackers. How about you take your walk, and when you get back we order a pizza or something through room service."

"Sounds good."

They walk through the doors, across the lobby floor, and to the elevator. Otto presses the button. They wait.

"What did you think of your Uncle Paul's place?"

"Pretty sweet," Robby says.

Otto points his finger at him. "Gotta work hard to make enough money for a place like that."

"I'll bet."

The elevator chimes and the doors open.

"I bet he'll come up to the camp," Otto says.

They step inside the elevator.

"I think I wore him down," he says, more to himself than to Robby.

Otto presses the button for the eighth floor. The doors close. The elevator rises.

~*~

Robby sits on a bench across the street from the downtown bookstore. Down the street, the lights on the State Theater look like a carnival. The title of the movie on the marquee is something in French. Families and couples walk along the sidewalk. People zip by on bikes or jog.

Robby has his phone next to his thigh on the bench. He looks at it, looks away, and then looks again.

Across the street, people come in and out of the bookstore. Through the window, he watches them browsing. In the bookstore's café a man drinks coffee and types on his laptop.

Robby's phone vibrates. He looks at the screen. It displays only a phone number with a 313 area code. He brings the phone up to his ear.

"Andre?"

"Yeah, it's me. Do you have my money?"

"I'm working on it."

"Is that why I'm calling you…so you can tell me that you're working on it?"

Robby rubs his palm on his pant leg. "Not exactly. I—"

"Where the fuck do you get off having that little weasel Tommy come down here and tell me that I need to call you?"

He switches the phone to his other ear. "It's just that I left town. I didn't want you to think...I mean, I'm not running. I'm not trying to take off or—"

"I don't give a shit what you're doing." He laughs. "You don't think I have other things to do than sit and think about some lowlife addict?"

He stands up. "I'm going to have—"

A family of four walks by. The daughter is about Robby's age and pretty. She looks at him and smiles.

He whispers. "I think I'll have about fifteen hundred for you."

Andre is quiet a moment before he speaks. "Double that, and you'll be fine. Everyone will be fine."

He walks into a pocket park and leans against a brick wall near a bicycle rack. "I just don't think that I'll be able to get the whole thing by—"

"This isn't a fucking negotiation."

He leans his head back against the wall and looks at the sky above Traverse City. "I just—"

"You have eleven days to get the rest of it. You know where to bring it. Fuck up, and I can't make any promises about what might happen."

"Andre..."

The other end goes dead.

Robby stares at his phone, the length of the last call still blinking on the screen. "Mother fucker."

~*~

Still holding his phone, he punches in another number. He paces while he waits.

"Hello, this is Tiffany."

"Hey, Tif—"

"I can't take your call right now. Leave a message and I'll get back to you as soon as I can. The beep's coming."

The phone beeps in his ear. He hangs it up and stuffs it down deep into his pocket.

He swings his hand backwards and raps his fist off the brick wall behind him.

He looks. The family from earlier is walking by again. They look away. The girl glances at him one more time, but doesn't smile.

~*~

Robby walks down Front Street. Most of the businesses—clothing stores, a toy store, a fly fishing shop—are closed. He glances through the windows of bars and restaurants or walks past their outdoor tables. People eat and drink and laugh. The street and sidewalks are busy with cars and pedestrians. He makes eye contact with nobody.

~*~

He crosses Union Street. The traffic thins, and there aren't nearly as many people on the street.

He keeps walking, his mouth silently talking to himself.

~*~

He stands on a bridge overlooking the Boardman River's darkness flowing below. It hums whisperingly. He holds his phone to his ear. In his other hand he holds a business card.

The other end of the line beeps.

"Yeah, hi," he says. "This is Robby Cooper. I'm supposed to meet with you tomorrow, but I wanted to let you know that I won't be there. I'm with my grandpa." He looks down at the dark water. "It's sort of an emergency. He can't drive, and he needed me to drive him somewhere, and we won't be back by tomorrow. I won't be there next week, either."

He squeezes his forehead in his hand. "I'm not slacking, just so you know. I mean, I know I've been kind of an asshole the last couple of times we met…I mean, just sitting there not saying anything, but I've started doing that daily accomplishment list. I'm not just saying that because I'm going to be missing a few sessions, either. I've really been doing it. I don't know, though. Some days it's a pretty short list."

He waits a moment while a couple walks past him. The woman has her head resting on the man's shoulder. They smile at him.

"Beautiful evening, isn't it?" the man says.

Robby nods. He lets them get a few yards beyond him.

"I know you want me to talk about my dad. That's probably the reason I've been so tight-lipped." He scratches at the corner of his eye. "I mean, I know this doesn't count as a session or anything, but... We were really close when I was younger, Dad and me. I was with him a lot. Then, I don't know, I got into the band in high school, and I guess I really started to blow him off. He called all the time trying to get me to go fishing or do something with him."

He closes his eyes and scratches his forehead.

"I don't even know really how it happened. I just kind of drifted away. At the end there, I guess we really weren't talking at all. I hadn't talked with him in over two months when he..." Looking up into the sky, he takes a deep breath and exhales it through pursed lips. "We were like best friends when I was younger, you know?" He sniffs and then catches himself. "It just leaves me feeling like I abandoned him, like maybe he—"

The other end of the line beeps. A woman's voice comes on: "Your message has reached its limit. Press 1 to send your message. Press 2 to review your message. Press 3 to record and send a new message."

He stares down at the water. He shakes his head and presses 3 on the keypad.

"Hey, this is Robby Cooper. I'm out of town for a family emergency, so I won't be there for Monday's session or next week's. I'll try to set up an appointment when I get back into town." He hangs up.

Lingering on the bridge for a moment, he turns and heads back in the direction of the hotel.

Robby and Otto sit at a table near a window eating pizza. From the Beacon Lounge on the tenth floor of the hotel, the scattered lights of Traverse City transition into the bruise-blue of the water and then the black of land in the distance. The lights of homes in the hills and along the shore of Grand Traverse Bay dot the western skyline.

Otto sets his piece on his plate and gazes out the window. "Your grandmother was right. Quite a view from up here." He clears his throat. "She would have loved it."

He studies his grandfather's rueful face. "Maybe she's seeing it right now through your eyes," he says.

Otto looks at him and smiles. "That would be something, wouldn't it?"

He nods.

Otto picks up his pizza and takes a bite. He looks out the window again and chews.

"Did you and Grandma ever stay with Uncle Paul when you came up here?"

He shakes his head. "He's only been up here for the last five years. He was at a hospital in Grand Rapids for a long time before that."

"What does he do?"

"Something in administration. I don't know what exactly, but he's a big wig."

Robby nods. "Yeah, looks like they pay him okay."

"He's scraping by, I guess," Otto says, smiling. He takes another bite.

"How did he end up working for hospitals?"

He shrugs. "Don't know. He went to Western for one of his degrees and then U of M after that for another one. Something with Business in it."

Robby leans back in his seat. "Looks like that's the way to go."

Otto works another piece off of the tray and onto his plate. "Paulie always had a head for the books. Classes came easy for him. Not like your Uncle Jack."

"Uncle Jack wasn't much for school?"

"Your Uncle Jack wasn't much for anything." He shakes his

head. "Paulie, though. He was scholarships all the way. That apple fell a long way from the tree when it comes to school. I used to joke with your grandmother that she must have had an affair with a bookworm mailman."

Robby laughs.

Otto takes another bite of pizza and then wipes his mouth with a napkin. "Has to be in his blood, too, because your Cousin Tyler was the same way. Smart as a whip when it came to school, just like his old man."

Robby squeezes his fist. A knuckle cracks.

"And I haven't seen a father and son get along like those two do. Best of buddies." Otto looks out the window into the night and shakes his head. "It's like they're not even from this family."

Robby looks down into his lap, taking a deep breath and long-sighing it out.

Otto looks back at him. "We should probably think about hitting the sack. This is a late dinner for me. My gut will probably be acting up all night."

He doesn't look up from his lap. "I'll probably go for another walk. This is early for me. I'm not really even tired."

Otto picks up his piece, but sets it back down again. "Why don't you just watch some TV in the room?"

"Nah," Robby says, looking up and meeting his grandfather's eye, "I just feel like taking another walk."

Otto looks at him until he looks away. "Why don't you just come back to the room? I won't be able to sleep until you get back anyway. I'll be waiting on edge for the door to open."

He stands up and shrugs a shoulder. "I'll just be like a half hour."

"Well, why you gotta—"

"Because, okay? Because I want to take a walk. Why's it have to be such a big deal?"

Otto waves both hands at him. "Fine. Jesus Christ, I don't care. Walk to Petoskey and back for all I care."

Robby turns to leave.

Otto looks at his watch. "A half hour, then. I'll see you at ten. Try to be quiet coming in too. I might manage to fall asleep."

Robby walks away from the table.

"Robby?"

"Okay," he says without turning back. "Ten. Whatever." He presses the button for the elevator that will take him down.

~*~

Robby stands in the parking lot of the hotel looking at the Firebird where it glows in a halo of luminescence under an overhead light. He rubs a finger thoughtfully along his upper lip.

He looks up at the hotel and then walks away toward the downtown.

~*~

Robby stands unsteady on the sand near where the dark water hishes quietly against the shore. Behind him a steady flow of traffic drones in both directions on East Grandview Parkway. He laces his fingers together and sets both palms on top of his head.

In the distance, the black of land sits at the far end of the black water.

He pulls his phone from his pocket and looks at the time.

12:17.

He sighs and puts the phone away. He looks back over his shoulder. The height of the hotel looms over the rest of the city's downtown. Its face is stippled with the pale yellow squares of light coming through the curtains.

He turns back to the water and reaches into his other pocket. He holds a small cylinder of darkness in his palm. Rolling it slowly between thumb and finger, he looks at it. The small tablets tumble against each other.

Behind him, the sound of steady footsteps scrape the asphalt. He stuffs the little container sharply back into his pocket.

Beyond the sand is grass and beyond the grass, a jogging path.

A silhouette jogs along the path. A man. He disappears and reappears in the slashes of light and dark coming through the trees. Robby keeps his back turned to him, but watches over his shoulder.

He waits until the silhouette fades, dissolved in darkness and distance. When it's gone, he turns and walks toward the towering hotel.

~*~

Robby slides out of the light of the hallway and into the darkness of the room. He holds the knob still twisted in his grip and only releases it once the door is closed. The strike latch whispers into the strike plate. He reaches down, unties his shoes, and leaves them on the floor of the cubby space that passes for a closet.

Otto's breaths are phlegmy, but rhythmic.

Robby pads lightly across the floor. Standing near his bed, he unzips his pants and pushes them down.

"Half hour, my ass. Where you been, boy?"

He startles. "Jesus. Just walking. Time must have gotten away from me."

"Well, you managed to wake me up."

He looks at his grandfather, a laid-out form of shadow in the next bed. "Sorry, Grandpa."

"Eh."

Robby pulls the comforter from the bed and lets it fall on the floor. He crawls in under the sheet and blanket.

"I don't care where you've been or what you've been doing, but we're getting on the road early tomorrow," Otto says into the half-darkness.

"Okay." He folds his pillow in half and rests his head on its doubled girth.

"Don't sass."

"Who's sassing? I said, 'okay'."

"I don't like the way you said it."

Robby exhales. "Goodnight."

"Just remember. Early. I don't want to hear any complaining."

"Got it."

"And watch that smart mouth, you hear?"

Robby sighs.

Otto snores lightly. Robby turns his head to the room's digital alarm clock.

2:47.

He rolls to his left side. After a moment, he rolls to his right. Then, he returns to his back.

He reaches onto the nightstand and picks up his phone. The screen glows back at him only the time. He sets it down again.

He pinches his lower lip again and again and stares up into the darkness of the ceiling.

~*~

Eight o'clock in the morning, the Firebird flies down M-72 toward Grayling. The sides of the highway are mainly scrub grasses and small evergreens. The view is a wash of olive, avocado, lime, jade and Kelly green.

Black road. The red car growling down its stretch.

Sunlight shines through the branches of the intermittent taller trees. Telephone lines run parallel to the road.

The Firebird's backend climbs a distant rise where the highway narrows, like a pencil lead coming to a point.

The car clears the rise and disappears, leaving only the land behind and the highway quieting as the engine's grumble fades out.

~*~

Robby and Otto wear waders standing in the grass behind the buildings of Gate's Au Sable Lodge. With its end plug on the ground, Robby's fly rod rests against his shoulder. Otto is close to him, watching his fingers. The main branch of the Au Sable river flows east past them. Its sound is a whispering, watery persistence.

"Good," Otto says, "now push the tip of the leader back through that loop."

His fingers follow Otto's words.

"Okay, good. Now don't pull it tight yet. Get some spit in your mouth first, and suck on the loop."

He looks at him. "What?"

"Just do it. The saliva cools down the monofilament. Otherwise the heat from the friction will weaken your knot." He laughs. "I broke off a lot of flies before I learned to suck on my knots."

Robby looks at him, grinning. "That's pretty gross, Grandpa."

He looks back. "Knots, I said. Knots."

Robby laughs, but then puts the loop in his mouth and moistens it. He takes it out a moment later and pulls it tight against the eye of the hook. He clips off the excess with the nippers dangling from his vest.

"Good," Otto says. "Now you can do mine. I got shit for eyes and shit for hands. I couldn't tie a decent knot if my life depended on it." He clenches and unclenches his thick fingers.

Studying it, Robby lets the fly with its red thorax and orange-black tail tumble about on its hackle in his palm. Otto moves next to him.

"Royal Coachman," he says, "There's not a much better fly for getting brookies to come up in the middle of the day. It's that red and green body. It's like Christmas to them…drives them crazy."

Robby lets go of the fly and it swings in the air at the end of his leader. He looks at the river flowing past in varying hues of whiskey browns and tans. "Why do they call it the Holy Waters?"

Otto takes a few steps toward the stream. "Because God put a little extra time into this stretch, boy," he says. "I don't think there's a better place to fish for trout in all of America…maybe all the world." He stands with his hands on his hips. Then he looks back. "So what do you think…you going to tie on my goddamn fly or what?"

~*~

Robby stands in the middle of the stream where the water is just over his knees. Above him, his fly rod ticks back and forth like the needle of a manic metronome. He releases his forward cast, and the line lands on the water in front of him, a tangle of spaghetti.

"No," Otto shouts from closer to the bank. "Keep your back cast behind you longer like I told you. Count to three before you start bringing it forward. You gotta give your line time to straighten out behind you."

He looks at his grandfather and exhales. "This is bullshit," he shouts, cupping his hand around his mouth. "Why don't you just fish by yourself?"

Otto shakes his head. "You're getting it. Just work on your back cast."

Robby glances at a property downstream. A couple sits on their dock watching him. The man leans forward and says something to the woman. The woman nods and takes a sip from her coffee mug.

"Come on. Come on," Otto shouts.

He looks up into the cloud-covered sky and then back at Otto. "I can't do it, Grandpa. Just fish by yourself, okay? I've been at it for almost forty-five minutes."

"Oh for Christ's..." Otto stops himself. Closing his eyes, he takes and releases a long breath. He opens his eyes again. "Hold on," he shouts. "Just wait there a second."

Picking his way carefully over the rocky bottom, he wades out toward the middle of river. When he gets to Robby, he stands behind him.

"What are you doing?"

He sets his left hand on Robby's left shoulder and takes his right wrist into his age-spotted right hand. "Let me work your arm, so you can feel what it's supposed to feel like."

"Grandpa..."

"Just hold the rod like I showed you. Firm, but not tight."

Holding Robby's wrist, Otto lifts it and the fly rod into the air, pulling both back to one o'clock. "One, two, three," he counts into Robby's ear and then brings the rod forward to eleven o'clock. "See, look how it straightens out. Now back." He pulls back again, guiding Robby's arm. "And then count. One, two, three."

The fly line loops and straightens behind them and then in front of them in a perfect rhythm, like a whip in slow motion.

"Can you feel how that's supposed to feel? Are you counting in your head on the back casts?"

Robby nods. "Yeah," he says, smiling.

Downstream, the man on the dock holds a camera. He takes pictures of them.

"Then, when you're ready," he says, bringing the rod forward, "just go to three o'clock and let the line lie down on the water."

In front of them, the line straightens and then drifts down to the surface. The leader unfurls the fly onto the water. It touches down like something whispered there.

"You see that? You had a strike."

Robby shakes his head.

"Doesn't matter. Just keep practicing your casting. You ready to try it on your own?"

He looks at the rod and then looks at Otto and nods.

Otto backs away from him toward the bank, watching. "You're going to hear guys telling you to cast between two o'clock and ten o'clock. That's too far. If you're back casting to one o'clock, the rod's going to naturally go to two o'clock anyway."

Back casting the line, Robby waits a moment, and then shoots it forward. The line straightens out in front of him and then touches down on the water. He looks at Otto. "Like that?"

"That's perfect, boy," he says. "Just remember, if something's wrong with your forward cast, the problem is in your back cast."

Robby casts again, the line singing a whistle over his head. He false casts it forward, retrieves it back again, and then sets down another flawless forward cast.

He looks at Otto, beaming.

Downstream, the couple applauds.

Robby looks at them. Then, he bows and smiles.

"Bravo!" the woman shouts, clapping harder.

"You goddamn ham," Otto says, laughing.

~*~

Robby and Otto stand in the river looking downstream. Near the end of a fallen cedar, a circle appears and then spreads out on the surface of the water. It floats away expanding and fading in the current.

"There he is," Otto says. "How long?"

Robby looks at his phone. "Right around a minute and a half again."

He nods. "Lot of times the bigger guys will get into a feeding pattern that's pretty close to clockwork. Right now he's on the bottom or under that cedar eating whatever he got. No sense casting to him for at least a minute."

He starts to walk downstream, moving his feet gingerly. "Go slow on your approach. Look at my feet."

Robby looks.

"I'm barely kicking up anything. See? Bunch of silt comes downstream...that lets the fish know that something is upstream in the water. That could end his feeding altogether."

Robby reads the surface ahead. "There was another rise farther down."

"That one will be yours. One fish at a time, boy." He raises his fly rod into a looping back cast and then drives it forward into a cast that lands several feet upstream from where the fish is feeding. "See that? Don't land the fly on top of the fish. Cast upstream and let it drift over him like any other bug on the river."

The Coachman glides in the current alongside the cedar. Near the end of the tree, it vanishes.

"Was that...?"

Otto lifts his rod and the tip bends over with the weight of the fish. "Just lift, don't yank," he says. "They have soft mouths. They're not like a bass." He winds in his slack line and then plays the fish on the reel. The line slices through the water toward the cedar.

He laughs. "Oh no you don't." He cranks the reel and pulls hard against the fish. "He's trying to snap me off in the branches."

The fish shoots toward the other side of the river. Otto turns with it. He staggers forward and almost falls into the water. "Damn it." He plants his feet. His fingers slip from the handle knob. The line goes slack a moment. He grips the knob again and begins to turn in line against the pulling of the fish. His face pales and he breathes heavily through his mouth.

Robby stares at the struggle.

Otto looks at him. "What are you gawking at, boy? Get your net ready."

~*~

Otto kneels in the water near the shore, his knees sunk in the gravel. The fish and his hands cupped gently around it undulate beneath the surface. Robby stands over his grandfather, watching. The fish's tail moves gently back and forth.

"Just have to let him recover a little. He'll be all right."

Robby watches. The fish drifts against one of Otto's palms, and then shifts from the touch. It doesn't swim away.

"Almost didn't get it. Haven't you ever netted a fish before?"

Robby shakes his head. "No."

Otto looks at him. "Not even with your old man when you were a kid?"

Robby wrinkles his nose. "He netted everything."

Otto looks back at the fish. "Gotta wait until the net's underneath him. Coming up too soon like you did, you can knock the hook right out of its mouth."

"Sorry."

"Well, no harm done. We got him. Must be close to twelve inches," Otto says. "Good size for a brookie." He looks up at Robby and smiles. "Of course, I'm not used to having anything quite this short between my legs."

Robby grins and shakes his head.

"You having a good time, boy?"

He looks at the river and smiles. "It's different. Peaceful."

"Sure is. Keeps your mind off things for a bit."

Looking away, he nods.

"Your old man sure loved it. I think he was up here every weekend most summers."

Robby squeezes his rod's cork grip. He looks down and moves his foot in the gravel bottom. "I should have gone when he—"

"Here he goes!" Otto pulls his hands away.

The fish snaps its tail twice and disappears into the blurry depths farther out.

After a moment, Otto holds out his hand. Robby pulls him groaning to his feet. He rests with his hand on Robby's shoulder. They both look downstream. The water moves around their legs.

Robby takes a deep breath and releases it from his mouth.

Otto rubs his back. "I miss him too, boy."

~*~

Robby stands in the bed of the river. The water flows around his hips. Near the bank, a great blue heron picks its way through the mud on spindly legs. Its head pivots on its S of a neck.

Robby looks downstream to where the river turns to the north. His grandfather's fly line sails backwards out of the bend, uncurls, and then flies forward again. When it comes into view thirty seconds later, it's only half as long.

After a few more casts, it's gone.

The heron stabs its head into the mud. A pair of frog legs dangles from its beak. It lifts its chin, and the legs disappear.

"You are gross," Robby says.

The heron looks, seemingly noticing him for the first time. It unfolds enormous wings and flaps itself up out of the mud and directly over his head. He watches it until it is out of sight over the trees.

Downstream, a fish rises in the middle of the river. Robby smiles. He waits for it to rise again. When it does, he starts toward it carefully, kicking up very little silt or gravel.

~*~

Robby's feet, rooted in the gravel of the riverbed, transition into his legs. His legs converge into his torso, which diverges again into his taut arms. His arms end at his hands gripping the fly rod. The fly rod bends to where the fly line passes through the last eye. The line, disappeared into the water, connects him to a violent resistance that he can't see.

~*~

Rounding the bend, Robby pushes through the water, smiling. He holds a six-inch brookie in one hand and his rod in the other. "Grandpa!" he shouts, looking around.

Farther down, the river turns another bend back to the south. He glances at the wilting fish in his hand. Its side is speckled with tiny puzzle pieces of yellow. The white under its jaw is repeated along the edges of its fins. With his palm under its belly and his fingers curled around it, he bends and holds it under the water. Its tail and fins move faintly.

Stooped over, still holding the fish beneath the surface, he lifts his chin and scans the river ahead. He squints.

Barely visible, his grandfather's legs jut out from the shore into the river.

He smiles. "Grandpa, wake up! I want you to see this. I got one."

Otto's legs rock in the movement of the surface near the shore. A bird flies from one side of the river to the other.

Robby stands up to his full height. The length of his grandfather's body lies in the shallow, muddy water. His head rests on the rocky shore, his eyes staring up into the overcast sky.

"Grandpa!"

It's a moment before Otto turns his slack face toward him. His mouth hangs open. He blinks, as though trying to bring Robby into focus.

He runs to him, kicking up great arcs of water.

Otto's mouth moves.

"What?" Robby asks.

He follows Otto's gaze to his own hand that still holds the limp brook trout. He tosses the fish into the river and kneels. "Are you okay? What's wrong?"

Otto doesn't make eye contact.

"Grandpa?"

His dilated eyes are on the fish. It floats on its side in the shallows, thrashing now and again, trying to right its body.

Robby looks at the fish and then back at Otto. "Grandpa, tell me what's wrong. What happened?"

Otto blinks. "...'ll die...can't breathe..."

"What are you...?" He slips his arms around Otto and lifts him into a hug. "Don't say that. Don't. You'll be okay." Tears stream down his cheeks.

"Wha...?"

Robby holds him tighter. "I said you're going to be okay."

Otto's mouth is close to his ear. "That fish…" he mumbles, "it won't live."

Robby looks at the fish floating on its side. A small tremor passes through it.

~*~

Robby crouches next to Otto where he leans against the trunk of a cedar tree. Behind him, the river whispers its movement.

Otto's legs are splayed out in front of him, palms flat on the ground. He opens his mouth, stretches his jaw, and then closes it again. He blinks. "Will you stop staring at me? I'm fine."

Robby shifts his weight to his other leg. "A couple minutes ago you couldn't tell me how many fingers I was holding up."

"Well now I can."

Robby scratches a spot of dried mud from his waders. "What happened?"

"I told you. I was going over to the bank to sit down and my foot got stuck in the mud. When I yanked it out, I fell. Must have hit my head on something."

"It was like you couldn't even understand what I was saying. You just kept going on about that fish."

"What fish?"

"The fish I caught—the one I threw back." He looks into his grandfather's pale face, into his pupils. "I think I should take you to the hospital."

Otto shakes his head. "I'm not going to the goddamn hospital. I feel fine." He crosses his arms. "Just give me a minute."

A few small songbirds land in the branches above them. They chirp and then flitter away.

"Does your head hurt?"

"Not bad…no. Let's not make a crisis out of this, okay? Old men fall down sometimes."

Robby scratches the back of his neck. "It's just that a doctor could tell—"

"You keep that shit up, and I'm going to give you a chance to see how many fingers I'm holding up."

"But, Grandpa—"

He points. "I'm serious, Robby. We're done talking about it."

They stare at each other until Robby looks at the ground.

Otto adjusts his back against the tree. "So you caught a fish?"

He nods.

"You like it?"

He looks up. "It was good."

"Well, you can keep the gear if you think you'll go again. I don't need two pairs of waders or two fly rods."

Robby picks up a handful of earth and then sifts it through his fingers. "I'd probably go again."

"Good. I can write down a few places where I used to go. You know, some secret spots. They wouldn't be hard to find if I drew you a map."

Robby shrugs. "Or we could just go together."

Otto nods, his eyes far away and thinking. "Well, sure. We could do that, too." He rubs his hand over his face and then rubs his palms together. "Why don't you help me up? I'm feeling just about a hundred percent."

Robby stands, and Otto holds out his arm. He pulls him to his feet.

"We'll go back to the lodge for a little dinner."

They stand at the river's edge. Otto starts into the mud at their feet. Robby walks to his side and holds his arm.

"Get off, now. I'm not a goddamn invalid."

The water climbs their legs as they move out into the river. They turn upstream and start against the current.

Otto stumbles forward and then catches himself. "Jesus Christ, I always forget how bad this part of fishing is. Rivers should flow downstream both ways."

They push against the current.

"You okay?"

Otto looks at him. "I'm going to pretend that you didn't ask me that," he says above the noise of the flowing water.

"Sorry."

They trudge forward. He watches his grandfather.

"Worry about your own feet."

"Sorry."

~*~

Robby stands in the gravel parking lot outside the entrance to Gate's Au Sable Lodge. He checks his phone and it shows that he has no service.

He looks across the lot at the Firebird where it shines in the sunlight coming in from the eastern sky. He studies it, working a finger back and forth across his upper lip.

"You're falling for the Bird, aren't you?" Otto says, coming through the door of the lodge. "You want her for yourself."

"What?"

"I saw the way you were looking at her."

Robby slips his phone into his pocket. "I was just thinking."

Otto shuffles past. "Well, you can think while you're driving. We're all paid up. Let's get on the road."

He glances at the car again and then follows his grandfather towards it.

~*~

The Firebird is parked in a driveway. A late Nineties model Ford Tempo is parked in front of it with one of its taillights covered in red tape. Robby and Otto sit looking at the house in front of them. It's a small, one-story ranch. The overgrown bushes in front of it look as though they haven't been trimmed in years. The moss-covered shingles on the roof are buckled and hunched.

The screen door to the house opens, and an overweight man wearing jeans and a t-shirt lurches out onto the stoop. His shirt is damp-dark at the armpits. The left side of his hair is matted to his head. His face looks moist. He holds a can of beer.

"Jesus, Jacky," Otto mutters.

Jack pushes his fingers through his hair. "Dad?" he asks toward the windshield of the car.

Otto opens his door and gets out onto the driveway. "Hey, Jacky."

Jack blinks. He then takes a pull from his beer before setting the can down on the stoop. He laughs. "Dad, what are you doing here?"

Otto closes his door. "Just came to see you."

Jack laughs again and shakes his head. "Holy shit. Never would have guessed that it was you out here." He walks down the stoop and across the patchy lawn.

Robby opens his door and gets out. Jack looks at him.

"Robby, too? It's a goddamn party!" He turns his attention back to Otto.

Otto holds out his hand. "It's been awhile."

Jack looks at the hand and starts laughing. "A handshake?" He throws his arms around his father and lifts him off the ground in a bear hug. "You're not going to get off with just a handshake."

"Okay, easy Jacky. My bones are getting a little brittle anymore."

Jack sets him down and holds his shoulders between his hands. He smiles. "I can't believe you're here." He looks at Robby. "Do you guys want something to drink?"

"Maybe coffee if you have it."

Jack laughs. "Shit, I don't even know if I do." He looks back at his house and then at them again. "I got beer. I know that much."

Otto shakes his head. "Jacky..."

"I mean, if Robby wants one." He nods in Robby's direction. "Maybe he wants one."

Robby shrugs.

"He's not old enough," Otto says.

"Well, come on in. I'll see what I have." He starts toward the house. Then, he stops. "Actually, if you don't mind, wait out here a second. Let me pick up a bit. I wasn't expecting company."

"You don't have to fuss on our account."

"It ain't fussing. I was going to clean up a bit this afternoon, anyway. I just hadn't got to it yet."

Otto nods. "We can wait."

Jack goes up the steps. He stops on the stoop with his hand on the door handle. He looks at them. "I just really can't believe that you're here. It's fu…it's crazy."

Otto smiles half-heartedly.

Jack glances at the beer can. He bends down, picks it up, and disappears into the house.

~*~

The white walls are yellowed with smoke. The carpeting in the living room looks as though it's never been vacuumed. Otto and Robby sit down on the sofa that is draped with a grimy bed sheet. They set their waters on the cut-down foosball table that serves as a coffee table. All of the rods with the little plastic soccer players have been removed.

Jack sits in a worn recliner across from them that is angled towards a large-screen television on the wall. He cracks open a beer and takes a long swallow.

Otto leans forward, reaches for his water, and takes a drink.

Robby looks at the muted screen that replays a Tigers game from the night before. In the top of the sixth, the Tigers are losing to the Yankees, eight to two.

"Fucking Yankees," Jack says. He takes a drink and then looks at Otto. "What?"

Otto quickly shakes his head. "Nothing."

Jack looks at Robby and then back to Otto. "You guys hungry? We could order a pizza."

"We had lunch before we came here," Otto says. "I was thinking, though, that I could take us all to dinner tonight."

Jack takes another pull from his beer. "Tonight? Like what time tonight?"

"Six o'clock or so…dinner time."

He shrugs. "I don't know. Maybe." He looks at Otto and smiles. "I'll tell you, Dad, you look pretty good. You look fit."

Otto looks down at himself. "I don't know…I feel like a bean pole."

Jack smacks his big belly with his open palm. "Not me."

Otto half-smiles and then reaches for his water. Robby does the same and takes a drink. Jack reaches into the ball catch of one of the goals on the foosball table. He pulls out a pack of cigarettes and a lighter.

"You still at Truck and Bus?"

Jack shakes a cigarette up from his pack and draws it out with his teeth. "It's GM Truck Group now but, yeah, I'm still there." He touches the flame of the lighter to the end of his cigarette. He takes a drag and exhales, staring at Otto. "The floor's getting retooled right now for a new model. The plant's shut down for the next couple weeks if you were wondering."

Otto sets his glass back on the table. "Wondering?"

Jack takes a drink. "Well, you were probably wondering what I was doing home in the middle of the day. Probably guessing that I was being a slacker."

Otto shakes his head. "Nope, I wasn't wondering. I'm just glad that you were here."

Jack takes a drag off his cigarette and turns his head to exhale. He turns back to face Otto. "So, what are you doing here, Dad?"

Otto rubs his palms on his pants leg and leans back into the couch. "Well, I wanted to ask—"

A cell phone plays "Bad to the Bone" in the kitchen.

Jack stands up. "Hold on, I'll be right back." He starts out of the room, but then turns back and grabs his beer.

Otto looks at Robby and smiles unconvincingly.

Jack's voice comes from the other room. "No, not right now." A moment passes. "I don't know, maybe tonight. Probably tomorrow, though. I've got some shit I have to do." Another moment. "I know, but something came up. I'll give you a call as soon as I can."

Otto squeezes one hand in the other.

"I will, man." Jack laughs. "No shit, it's going to be a good time."

Robby looks at Otto and starts to get up. "I'm going to go outside and make a phone call."

Otto pumps a halting palm at him. "Just keep your pants on."

Robby sits again.

A moment later, Jack walks back into the room and falls into his seat. He opens a fresh beer and takes out another cigarette. "So, what'd you want to ask me, Dad?"

Otto scoots forward on the cushion. Robby crosses his arms.

~*~

Jack sits low in the recliner with a lit cigarette hanging from his lips. He scratches his head. "And Paulie already said that he was going to go?"

"It felt like that was the way we left it," Otto says. "He'll come up on Saturday. Maybe you could ride up together."

Jack laughs. "Yeah, that will happen." He takes a drag of his cigarette and exhales it above the foosball table.

"You said that you don't have work for the next couple of weeks," Otto says. "I'm just talking about a weekend."

He tilts his beer to his lips and drains the can. He sets it on the arm of his chair. It falls clanging to the floor. "Paulie actually said he's going?"

"Like I said, it sounded like that was the way he was leaning."

Robby looks at Otto, but Otto's attention is focused on Jack. "You could call him for a ride."

Jack looks at him and blinks his soupy eyes. "My car'll make it."

"Oh, sure," Otto says. "It was just an idea."

"Grand Marais," Jack says. He points at Otto, but moves his finger toward Robby. "Down in Grand Marais," he sings. "Down in Grand Marais...yeah." He laughs.

An uncertain, almost sympathetic smile curls Robby's lips. He nods.

Jack smiles, too. "You know that tune, man? That's a good fucking tune. You know who sang that?"

Robby nods. "The Animals. That's 'Monterey'."

Jack snaps a mushy snap and points his finger at him. "That's right." He keeps his finger pointing. He blinks. "Look at Gerry's boy with all the answers."

"Jacky?"

Jack jerks his head toward Otto. "What?"

He crosses his arms and shrugs a shoulder. "What do you think...about Grand Marais this weekend?"

Jack stands up, sways around the table, and heads for the kitchen. "Shit, I'll go. Why not?" he says, before disappearing from the room.

The sound of him opening another beer cracks from the kitchen.

Otto turns his head over his shoulder. "Jacky?"

"Yeah?" he calls.

Otto inhales and then exhales. "I can't have you bringing any booze up there."

Holding his beer, Jack appears, leaning in the doorway between the two rooms. "What?"

He looks at him and shakes his head. "I'm going to need you sober."

He staggers into the room, his neck flushing red up to his ears. "You're fucking kidding me."

"It's just a weekend, Jacky."

Robby stares into the couch.

After a moment, Jack laughs. "You're asking me to stay sober for a weekend? When the fuck did you ever stay sober for a weekend?"

Otto looks at his hands. "You're right." He looks up. "But that was a long time ago now, Jacky."

"Uncle Jack—"

"Shut up, Robby." Jack takes a drink of beer. He smiles spitefully and shakes his head. "You don't even want me to go."

"Jacky—"

"What? You don't. You wanted to go up there with little rich bitch Paulie. He's your fucking golden boy now. That's why you went up to his place first…to make sure he was going. No Paulie, no trip." He hooks his thumb into the top of his pants and staggers a step to his right. "You're only inviting me out of guilt."

He shakes his head. "Jacky, that's not true."

"Bullshit it isn't. You've been looking down your nose at me since you got here. Ol' lazy ass Jacky is all you see. Shitty car. Shitty house. Shitty life. I turned out just the way you thought—"

Otto crosses his arms. "Goddamnit, Jacky, I'm trying to invite you to come up to the cabin with me. If you'd stop whining for a minute maybe you'd figure that out."

Jack stares at him. "You know what…get the fuck off my couch."

"Jacky."

"I'm serious, Dad. Get the fuck out of here." He turns a glare toward Robby. "And take little piss face with you."

After a moment of staring, he pitches his beer can at him. Robby jerks his arms and knees in to cover his middle. The can, half full, crashes against his forearm, sending a shower of beer all over him. He leaps to his feet.

"What the hell, Uncle Jack?"

"Fuck you, Gerry."

Robby slap-brushes at the beer on his shirt and pants. "What?"

Jack raises his fists. He wobbles and then regains himself. "Do something you little piss ant. Just take one step." He looks at Robby's fists clenched at his side and goads him forward with his fingers. "Right now, you little fucker. Take your best—"

Otto stands up in between the two of them. He stares into Jack's face. "Go out to the car, Robby," he says without turning.

"Yeah, pussy, go out to the—"

Otto sticks his finger in Jack's face. "That's enough, goddamnit. You shut your mouth now, Jacky. Robby didn't do a damn thing to you."

Jack's lips buckle in against his teeth. After a moment, he looks at the floor.

"Go on now, Robby," Otto says.

Jack's face melts. He looks close to tears. "Robby, I'm sorry. Jesus Christ…"

Robby weaves around the foosball table and out the front door.

Otto opens the driver's side door. Robby looks up at him.

"Push over. I'll drive."

After a moment, Robby climbs over to the passenger's side. Otto gets in and pulls the door closed. He looks through the windshield at Jack's front door. Hands on the wheel, he takes a long breath and exhales it slowly.

"Keys."

Robby lifts his hips from the seat, digs down in his pocket, and negotiates the keys carefully out. He sets them in Otto's hand.

Otto jangles them in his palm until he finds the key he wants. He puts it in the ignition, but doesn't start the car. Instead, he holds the steering wheel in both hands and stares again at Jack's house. "I'm sorry for what happened in there."

Robby lifts his beer-soaked shirt away from his skin. "It wasn't your fault, Grandpa."

"Not everyone would agree with you about that, boy."

"What?"

Otto looks at him and smiles half-heartedly. "Nothing." He looks back at the house. "He'll probably sleep it off now."

"I hope so. He went nuts."

Otto nods. "He's always had a short fuse, but he's mostly bluff."

Robby looks at the house, too. Then he looks at Otto. "Do you think he'll come up to Grand Marais?"

He shakes his head. "I doubt it. When I told him one more time that I really wanted him to go, he told me that I could rot in hell." He reaches down and turns the ignition. The engine growls and then idles.

He shifts into *reverse* and throws his arm across the back of his seat. He looks over his shoulder. After a moment of staring, he turns around and shifts the car back into *park*. He stares at the house. Then, he looks at Robby. "You drive, okay? I don't know what the hell I was thinking." He shakes his head and sighs. "This whole thing has been a bust. We should probably just go home."

Robby gets out. Walking around the back end of the Firebird, he studies his uncle's house, nibbling his lower lip. He stands for a moment in the wedge of space behind the open driver's side door, looking thoughtful.

~*~

Still wearing his clothes and shoes, Otto lies on top of the bed's comforter watching the news with the sound off. His eyes close, snap open, and then close again. Robby sits in a chair near the window. He watches his grandfather until the old man's eyes don't open again. His light, raspy breathing fills the room.

Robby looks out the window at the Firebird in the light of the motel's parking lot. He studies it for a long time.

Beyond it, headlights and taillights stream east and west on I-69 and north and south on I-75.

Robby looks at Otto. His eyes are open again.

"Grandpa?"

Otto turns his head toward him. "What?"

"Is it alright if I go out? I got a friend down in Fenton I might stop in on."

He scratches his bushy eyebrow. "Why don't you just go to bed?"

"Grandpa, it's ten o'clock."

He waves a hand at him. "I don't care, boy. Knock yourself out." He points. "But don't even think about drinking and driving in that car."

Robby hops up and scoops the keys from the bedside table. "I won't."

Otto reaches into his pocket and tosses a room key to the end of his bed. Robby grabs it on the way by.

"Don't be out all night, either."

"I won't."

Robby opens the door to the room. He looks back. Otto is laid out on the bed, eyes closed again.

"Robby?"

He stops.

"Don't do anything stupid."

Robby swallows. "I won't."

~*~

The porch light is off or burned out. Robby stands in the dark on the stoop, waiting. The open screen door rests against his shoulder. Television light flickers in the front window.

He looks at his cell phone screen and then slips it back into his pocket. He presses the doorbell and then knocks.

Behind him, a car with a failing muffler and one headlight sputters down the street. He looks over his shoulder at it and then turns back. He knocks again.

The door opens. His Uncle Jack stands in the dim light squinting at him. His eyes are puffy, and he's in a t-shirt and boxer shorts. "Who is it?"

"Hey, Uncle Jack."

"Robby?" Jack edges more of his body behind the wooden door. "What are you doing here?"

He crosses his arms. "I just want to talk."

Jack looks at him and blinks. "I'm sorry for throwing that beer. I was drunk."

"That's not what I want to talk about," he says, shaking his head. He uncrosses his arms and stuffs his hands in his pockets. "Is it okay if I come in?"

Jack looks past him into the driveway and then back into his face. "I was going to go to bed soon."

"It won't take long."

Jack takes a step backwards and pulls the door open wider. "Yeah, come on in. Just don't sucker punch me or anything. I already have a fucking headache."

Robby crosses the threshold and goes in past his uncle.

~*~

Robby sits at Jack's kitchen table with a beer in front of him. When he lifts his feet, they stick slightly to the floor before coming free. Jack sits across from him taking slow sips from his own beer. The only light in the room comes from the range's hood.

Robby picks up his beer and takes a drink. He sets it back down. "Otto would be pretty pissed if he knew I was drinking a beer and then planning to drive his car."

Jack squeezes two dents into his can. "Yeah? Well, he's no saint himself. How the hell did he talk you into carting his ass all over the place?"

Robby looks at the table. "He's paying me."

"Paying you?" Jack squeezes the can from another direction, and the original dents pop back out. "Why?"

"I asked him to. I need the money."

Jack nods slowly. "Well, good. Nobody should have to spend time with that asshole for free."

Robby skates the tip of a finger over the surface of the table. He watches it do figure eights. "That seems a little harsh."

"Does it, Robby? Does that seem a little harsh?" He takes a drink of beer and strikes the bottom of the can against the tabletop. "You know, you shouldn't talk about shit that you don't know anything about." He looks at his beer can. "Otto is a prick sonuvabitch. Period."

Robby looks into his lap and massages his fingers over his forehead.

"You're the spitting image of little Saint Gerald right now."

Robby looks up.

Jack laughs. "Anytime I bad-mouthed Otto, your old man would get the same look on his face. Like I was making those stories up or something." He takes another swig of beer.

"People change, Uncle Jack."

"That doesn't mean anything." He picks up his can, wiggles it, and then sets it back down on the table. Getting up, he goes to the refrigerator and takes out another. He pulls the tab. "I used to date this woman for a while. Any time she'd see an old man, she'd say, 'Look at that little cutie. What a sweetheart.' Like the guy was a fucking kitten or something." He takes a drink. "Sure as fuck isn't what I think when I see an old man. When I see an old man, I think, 'You aren't fooling me, geezer. You were probably a bastard your whole life. You're only mellow now because you know people would kick your wrinkly ass if you tried to pull that shit again.'"

"Uncle Jack…"

"What? I'm serious." He comes back to the table and sits down. "You look at Otto now—looking like an old Jimmy Stewart—you wouldn't guess even one tenth the shit he pulled back in the day. It was almost like he planned it…like he woke up in the morning and thought, 'Okay, how can I be an asshole today?'"

Robby takes a drink of his beer. A June bug buzzes against the screen of the window over the sink and then flies away.

Jack reaches under his shirt and scratches his belly. "Alright, here's a little gem for you. Classic Otto." He shakes his head. "We used to have a lot of problems with water in the basement when Paulie and me were little kids. Almost every other spring, water would come up and seep in under the cinder blocks of the foundation. Sometimes we'd have an inch or two of standing water. Dad got sick of hiring guys to come out and snake the drain tiles under the house, so he bought the equipment to do it himself." He shakes his head. "Then he decided that since he had the equipment, he might as well make some money from it. He bought an old piece of shit truck and ran an ad in the newspaper every spring. I still remember what he called it...Ottomatic Drain Repair." Jack makes a horse-like sound with his lips. "Only thing automatic about it was that he had two slaves to do all the work for him.

"Whenever he'd get a call, he'd take me and Paulie with him. The first couple of times, we just helped him. He showed us how to do it. It makes me sick, but those are some of the best memories I have of being with the guy. He was talking nice to us, teaching us stuff. We didn't know that his plan was to start dropping us off at houses by ourselves." He takes a long drink of beer and sets the empty can on the table. "Pretty soon, he'd only be there long enough to talk to the people and set up the job. After that, he'd leave us standing in the driveway with the equipment." He shakes his head. "It was heavy shit, too. That power feed cleaner had to be over 100 pounds."

Jack gets up and lurches to the refrigerator. "That first spring I think I was thirteen years old." He looks up and squints an eye. "That would have made Paulie fifteen." Beer in hand, he closes the refrigerator. "You see what I'm saying? That sonuvabitch left us by ourselves with two or three hours of work on our hands, and then he went to the bar to watch a ballgame and drink." He sits down, takes a long drink, and then looks at Robby. "You smoke?"

Robby shakes his head.

"Health nut, eh?"

He shrugs. "I just don't smoke is all."

"Shit. I was just about to run out and get a pack before you got here." He gets up and goes through the doorway into the living room.

Robby looks at a framed picture on the wall to the left of the stove. It's a drawing of an owl on a branch.

"Like that?" Jack says, coming back into the room. He talks around a half-smoked cigarette in his mouth. The end is blackened where it was mashed out in an ashtray earlier. He sits and then sets two other cigarettes like the one between his lips on the table. "I drew that."

Robby looks closer. "That's pretty good."

"I made it for Otto when I was a kid. Found it in a drawer down in his workshop under a bunch of owner's manuals." He shakes his head. "Another one of my treasured memories. I took it with me when I moved out since he didn't seem to give two shits about it."

"Maybe he looked at it when he was working on stuff."

Jack flips a flame up to his cigarette. "Give me a break, will ya? Jesus Christ, like father like son." He takes a drag and kinks an eyebrow. "What was I talking…oh yeah, the drain tiles. Do you want to know how much he charged to snake out a basement? Three hundred bucks." He laughs. "That's why nobody ever asked any questions about him letting two teenagers do the work. His prices were too good." He looks at him and points. "Take a guess how much he paid us."

Robby shakes his head.

"Ten bucks a piece. Ten bucks! Then he'd come at us with shit like, 'How much money do you guys need at your age, anyway?' and 'Who do you think pays for that food you eat every day?' and 'That's a helluva lot more than my old man ever gave me for helping him cut and deliver firewood. You want to know how much he paid me? Nothing. When I told my old man that I was done cutting wood, he put me out of the house. Seventeen years old, and I was out on my own,'" he says, in a voice meant to mimic Otto's. He shakes his head. "It was never any use to complain to him because he always had a harder luck story that could trump the shit out of yours."

Robby nods. "My dad told me that Otto had a pretty rough childhood."

"Yeah, yeah, yeah. So that makes everything okay. Otto had it tough, so we have to forgive him that there were times that he forgot to pick us up and we had to walk home dragging all that shit behind us, only to find out that he'd fallen asleep in his truck after tying one on at the bar." He flicks his ash on the floor. "Poor fucking Otto." He takes another long drink.

"I think he's sick."

Jack drops his cigarette into his beer can. It hisses out in the bottom. He looks at Robby. "Sick, my ass. That old sonuvabitch is probably healthier than both of us."

"I don't think so."

Jack rolls one of the cigarettes on the table back and forth. The end leaves a little black trail. Then, he gets up and goes to the refrigerator. He stands in the light of the open door. "Okay, I'll bite. What makes you think he's sick?" He comes back to the table and cracks open the beer in his hand.

"We were fishing yesterday and—"

"Fishing? He took you fishing? That fuck never—"

"Uncle Jack, he fell. I found him lying on the bank. I thought he was dead. When I got to him, he wasn't making any sense at all. He was babbling, like he was crazy or something. It scared the hell out of me."

Jack picks up another mangled cigarette and fits it between his lips.

"Then, when we got back to the lodge, he went to bed. He slept from four in the afternoon until nine the next morning. I mean, I don't know, maybe he had a minor heart attack or something." Robby shakes his head. "For a while I just sat on the other bed and watched him breathe. I swear, I thought he was going to be dead the next morning."

It takes Jack a moment to guide the flame to his butt. "Why didn't you take him to the hospital?" he asks, talking out a mouthful of smoke.

"He wouldn't let me."

"Well, he looked alright to me today."

Robby scratches his chin. "If he's okay, then why is he having me drive him everywhere? He told me that his doctor doesn't want him driving."

Jack looks across the table at him with glassy eyes.

"Uncle Jack?"

Jack points. "Beer no good?"

"What? No, it's fine. I just don't feel like drinking."

Jack takes a drink of his own beer. "So, you think he's pretty sick?" he slurs.

"I don't know. I think he could be."

Jack has a hiccup that turns into a belch. "That what you came here to tell me?"

He nods. "Yeah, I guess so."

Jack laughs. "When I saw you at the door, I figured you wanted to kick my ass for throwing that beer at you."

He shakes his head. "No. It wasn't that big of a deal."

Jack nods. "Anyway, that would have been a mistake on your part. I might look like shit, but I can still throw down."

"I bet."

Jack takes a long pull from his can. "So, what do you think...you think I should head up to Grand Marais?"

Robby nods. "If you have the time."

Jack leans back in his chair. He takes a drink and then looks at the microwave. "You want to watch some TV?"

Robby is quiet for a moment. Then, "Sure."

Jack reaches down into his pocket and pulls out a crumpled ten-dollar bill. He sets it on the table. "Run out and get me a pack of smokes, will ya? I'll throw a frozen pizza in the oven for us."

"Okay." Robby smiles. He takes the ten and, smoothing it with his fingers over the table, works it back into shape.

~*~

Robby pushes a door open. The light from the hallway shines in on an unmade bed. His Uncle Jack is slouched against him.

"I'da been fine in the chair."

Robby staggers him into the room. "You'll sleep better in here."

He rolls him onto the bed. Untying one of his shoes, he pulls it from his foot.

"You're alright, Robby boy," Jack mumbles. "You're a…a good kid."

He pulls off his other shoe. "Just get some sleep."

"I will."

Robby folds as much of the comforter as he can around his uncle.

"Don't be mad at me. I'm sorry about everything. I'm sorry."

"I'm not mad, Uncle Jack."

Jack reaches out for him. "Shake my hand."

Robby takes his hand. They shake. Jack doesn't let go.

"I didn't even ask. How's your mom? She good?"

"She's okay."

Jack starts pumping his hand again. "I always liked her. Tell her I said hi, will ya? Will ya do that?"

"I'll tell her." He gets his hand away from his uncle's grip.

The hand drops to the mattress. "Your old man put her through some shit."

Robby crosses his arms and shrugs. "What do you mean?"

"You don't do that to someone. Not someone…not someone like her." He rolls on his side toward the wall. "She was always good to him," he slurs. "She didn't deserve to be treated like…not by that two-faced sonuva…"

He stares at his back. "Uncle Jack?"

Jack rolls the other way and stands out of bed. "I'm going to throw up." Hand over his mouth, he bolts from the room and pounds down the hallway. The bathroom door slams shut. Jack hacks the watery contents of his stomach into the toilet. After a moment, he releases another salvo.

Robby stands in the dimly-lit bedroom. Then, he goes to the door and looks down the hallway.

Jack spits repeatedly. His voice comes through the closed door. "Jesus Christ."

"You okay, Uncle Jack?"

"I'm fine." He gasps a wheezy, open-mouthed breath. "You can go. I'll be fine."

Robby starts down the hallway and then turns back. "I'll see you up at the cabin, okay?"

Jack vomits again.

Robby walks to the front door and out into the darkness.

~*~

Robby drives west on I-69. In the distance, a plane spotted with lights makes its descent into Bishop Airport. He takes his phone from his pocket and looks at the glowing list of his contacts. He slides his thumb, looking from the screen to the road and back to the screen. He stops on Tiffany's name and then touches the screen again.

After a few rings, he listens to her voice. "...as soon as I can. The beep's coming."

"Hey, Tif, it's Robby. It's probably a little late for me to be calling. You said that I should give you a call from the road, so I am. Give me a call back when you get a chance."

He hangs up and then scrolls through his contacts again.

He stops on *Mom*.

For a moment, he drives with one hand on the wheel and the other holding the phone. Then, he presses *End* and tosses the phone on the passenger seat.

~*~

When he slides the key through the reader, the green light flashes. He turns the knob slowly and drifts open the door.

Wearing boxer shorts and a t-shirt, Otto stands in the light of a lamp sifting through the clothes in Robby's luggage.

Robby touches his pants pocket. Then, "Grandpa?"

Otto jumps and turns to him. "Jesus Christ, you scared the hell out of me." He looks again at the bag and then at Robby. His face calculates. "You got any toothpaste in here? I can't find the goddamn toothpaste."

"It's in the bathroom."

He crosses his arms. "Where in the bathroom? I didn't see it."

Robby reaches in and flips on the bathroom light. The toothpaste sits next to the sink. He points. "Right there."

Otto shakes his head. "I swear I must be losing my marbles. I looked in there twice."

"With your eyes open?"

He takes a pair of pants and a shirt from the floor and stuffs them back into Robby's bag. "Don't be a smartass." He glances at the clock. "Where the hell have you been, anyway? It's after one in the morning."

Robby crosses his arms. "My friend wasn't around. I went to Uncle Jack's."

"Uncle Jack's?" He lowers himself into a chair near the room's table. "What the hell did you go there for?"

Robby pulls off one of his shoes and then the other. "Just to talk."

"To talk."

He nods.

"What did you talk about?"

Robby walks over and sits on his bed. "Nothing much. Grand Marais, I guess."

"Grand Marais?"

He nods.

"What did you say about Grand Marais?"

"I don't know. Just that he should go. It sounds like he might."

"He said that?"

"More or less."

Otto sits in the chair. He scratches his nose. "You talk about anything else?"

"Not really. We watched some TV."

He sniffs a little laugh. "Regular boy's night out, eh?"

"I guess so."

Otto nods and then pushes himself to standing. "How drunk did he get?"

Robby unbuttons and then unzips his pants. "Not too bad, really. Just a few beers."

"You drink too?"

"Half a beer."

Otto climbs into his bed. "And then you drove my car?"

"I'm pretty sure I was under the legal limit."

"Yeah. Probably." He pulls the blanket up around himself and lays his head on the pillow. "Well, I suppose we should get to sleep. It will take us a day or two to get the cabin ready for company. Got a bit of a drive tomorrow, too."

Robby finishes undressing and then turns off the lamp before getting into his own bed. "Grandpa?"

"Yeah?"

"Didn't you want to brush your teeth?"

A moment passes before he answers. "Eh, I'll just do it in the morning. I've been up most the night waiting for you, boy. I'm bushed."

Robby stares into the ceiling. "Sorry."

"You're forgiven. Now get some sleep."

~*~

Robby stands with his phone to his ear outside of Audie's restaurant in Mackinaw City. Cars stream past on I-75 in front of him. North of him, the south side tower of the Mackinac Bridge juts white into the blue sky. He walks across the parking lot and leans against the Firebird.

"He shouldn't have said that," his mom says on her end of the call.

"He was drunk," Robby says. "I doubt he remembers saying it."

A stiff wind blows across the parking lot. Robby huddles into himself.

"Did you have a good time fishing with—"

"What did he mean, Mom? What was Uncle Jack talking about?"

She sighs. "It's nothing that you need to know anything about."

He pushes his hand through his hair and looks at the asphalt. "He made it sound like Dad cheated on you."

She doesn't say anything. Another gust of wind blows across the parking lot. Robby shivers.

"Mom?"

She sighs again. "Your father had problems. I don't think he could help—"

"Who was she?"

"Robby, you don't need to—"

"Who, Mom?"

A couple in their forties comes out of the restaurant, pulls their jackets tight around them, and rushes across the lot to their car.

"They. What you want to ask is, 'Who were they?' It wasn't something that only happened once."

He slouches a little lower against the car. "What?"

"He didn't want to be that way," she says. "He really didn't."

He clears his throat. "When did you know?"

"Robby, I really don't think you need to know all the—"

"When did you know?"

A moment passes. "The first time was really early in our marriage...before you were even born. It was a woman that he worked with."

Robby looks up and to the south where the gigantic white blades of a wind turbine slice gracefully through the air. "You didn't leave him?"

"After I found out, we went into counseling. I still loved him. I wanted to try to save our marriage. So did he." She sniffs a breath. "We were better after the counseling. It wasn't too long after that that I was pregnant with you."

Robby switches the phone to his other ear.

"Being a father meant everything to him. He was good for a long time after you were born. He would come home on his lunch breaks to give you baths. If you woke up at night, he'd always take you downstairs so I could sleep. I'd hear him singing to you." She pauses. "Those are some of my favorite memories of our marriage."

"But then he did it again?"

She says nothing for a moment. "You were older then...starting school. There was a change at work, too. He was traveling more. He was one of their best salesmen, so they started sending him all over the place. For somebody with his issues, it was the perfect storm."

Shivering, Robby gets inside the car and then closes the door. "How did you find out?"

"I guess I just knew. He was distant again like he had been the first time. I didn't have any proof, but I knew."

He touches his fingers over the radio knobs. "That's when you decided to leave him?"

"I didn't. Not right away. I was afraid of the idea of being a single mother. I didn't have any work skills or anything. I was totally dependent on him."

He pushes through the preset buttons absently. "Is that when you went back to school?"

She makes an affirmative noise in her throat. "Even while I was in school, I tried to make things work. I tried to be a really good wife to him. I guess I was trying to win him back...trying to get him to see everything that he had. Sometimes I'd even try to convince myself that I was just being neurotic...that maybe his seeming distant was only a symptom of him traveling so much. Even while I was taking classes, there were times when things seemed better between us, but by then I'd found out that I really liked school. At that point I wouldn't have quit even if I'd had proof that he wasn't cheating."

He switches ears again. "Did you ever have proof...that he was cheating?"

"I did. I guess in a way I wasn't the only one he was cheating on. One of the women had really fallen for him. He'd been telling her that he was going to leave me and marry her. Then she found out that there were other women besides her. She got our home number and called me and told me that she'd been having an affair with him for close to a year. She made it seem like she was trying to be good to me by letting me know the truth, but I'm sure she was doing it out of spite."

He looks out the windshield toward the entrance of the restaurant. "Is that when you left him?"

"That's when I confronted him. You probably don't even remember, but I sent you to Grandpa and Grandma's—"

"I remember."

She's quiet a moment. "I suppose you would."

He flicks a finger against the glove box. "I came home, and Dad was staying in a motel. I thought it was something I did. I thought that's why you sent me to Grandpa and Grandma's...because you were talking about me." He swallows.

"About you?"

"Don't you remember? I'd gotten into those fights at school during lunch. And then I had that three-day suspension because I got caught skipping class."

"You thought we were talking about you?"

He closes his eyes. "What was I supposed to think? I was in sixth grade. You didn't tell me anything…just that you and Dad were splitting up."

"Oh, honey, it wasn't about you. It wasn't about you, at all. We were—"

"What did he say?"

She's quiet a moment. "What, honey?"

"What did he say when you confronted him?"

She takes a breath. "He started to cry. He told me that he was sick and needed help. When I kept pressing him, he told me everything…that there'd been many women. Dozens…" She takes another breath. "Robby, I really don't want to talk about this anymore, okay? That's all in the past. I really don't think about it anymore, and I don't want to."

He leans his head back and looks up into the car's pristine headliner. "I just wanted to know what Uncle Jack was talking about."

"Well, now you know. I don't want this to change how you feel about your father. I don't—"

"That's pretty impossible."

"What he did was between the two of us. He was a good father to you. He was always trying to give you—"

He squeezes his free hand into a fist. "It wasn't just between the two of you."

"I suppose you're right. He did always try, though…to be there for you. Even after the divorce he made an effort to be a good father to you."

"I wonder sometimes if I was a good son."

"Honey…"

"I shut him out. I barely talked to him or did anything with him those last couple years."

"Robby—"

He sniffs in a breath. "It makes me think sometimes that maybe he—"

"Don't even say that. That's not fair to yourself to even think it. Your father had a lot of demons."

He looks out the windshield again. "Did you ever forgive him?"

"I made a peace with that part of my life, so I suppose I did."

"Did you ever tell him that you forgave him?"

"No. And I don't think I owed him that either. And, I really don't know if I forgave him or just put that part of my life away."

Otto opens the door to the restaurant and starts toward the car. He stops and zips up his coat. Then he fingers the zipper of his crotch.

"I have to go, Mom."

"Now wait a minute. I still wanted to talk to you about—"

"Everything's okay, Mom. I'm good, but I got to go." He hangs up the phone and turns off the ringer.

Otto opens the passenger door and looks down at him. "Did you forget which one of us is the chauffer, boy?"

Robby gets out of the car and walks around to the driver's side. He gets in. He doesn't start the car.

"What's that look for? I told you that I might be awhile."

"Nothing." He takes a long breath and then exhales it. He turns the engine over.

"Are you pretty regular?"

Robby looks at him. "What?"

Otto shifts his ass on the seat and winces. "Can you take a crap when you want to take a crap?"

He laughs. "Yeah."

"Well, don't take it for granted. Appreciate every one of them. Time's going to come when you can't, and it's its own special kind of hell. Puts a whole new spin on the phrase 'bound and determined.'"

Robby shifts into drive, smiling. "Jesus Christ, Grandpa."

He closes his eyes and puts his head back against the rest. "You'll pray to him, too, but most times that won't help, either."

~*~

They rise up the south side anchorage toward the first tower of the bridge. The straits are blue beneath them. Across the water, the Upper Peninsula stretches green to the west. Robby looks to his right. Mackinac Island is another mass of land in the eastern distance. A freighter in the middle of the straits is a brown smudge with churning white water behind it. A Star Line ferry races toward the Island, shooting up a rooster tail of spray from its backend. The white clouds appear brush-stroked into the blue sky.

With both hands on the wheel, Robby drives the Firebird on the grated middle lane. It hums beneath them.

"You like ruining my tires, boy?"

"It's not ruining your tires." He motions his head. "I just can't drive in that other lane, not close to the railing like that."

Otto sits up and looks out the window. "You been up to the Yoop before?"

He shakes his head. "Dad talked about taking me, but I never went."

Otto nods. "It's different. People make a pretty big deal about it. Lots of scrubland for the most part, but the big lake is something to see." He shrugs. "It's all pretty pure, I guess. Pretty untainted."

The Firebird passes the second tower and descends toward the toll booths.

Robby holds the wheel. "Did my dad ever go up to the cabin while he and my mom were married...by himself?"

"I don't know. Maybe. Why?"

He shakes his head. "No reason."

He pulls into one of the lines edging its way toward one of the booths.

"Welcome to the U.P., boy. If anybody asks you up here, you're a fan of the Packers."

~*~

Leaning his body against the driver's side door, Robby rests the side of his head in his folded arms on the Firebird's roof. He stares east. The car is parked on the shoulder of M-28 at the crest of a long rise. The shadows of trees stretch across the asphalt, and the highway reaches its vanishing point in the blue-green distance.

Not far from the car, a robin touches down in the middle of the highway. It bounds a few steps, pivots its head from side to side, and then flies off into the trees.

"You sleeping or what?"

Robby looks toward the trees, resting his chin on his bicep. Zipping his fly, Otto shuffles toward him through the long grass along the side of the road.

Robby smiles. "Prostate problems and constipation? You're a wreck."

Otto steps onto the gravel. "Yeah, yeah, yeah. It's pretty funny to make fun of old people, isn't it, boy?"

He stands up straight and stretches his arms over his head. "Sometimes."

Otto comes around to the driver's side and looks down the road. He points. "See that bridge at the bottom of the hill?"

Robby sees the bridge and then nods.

"That's where the East Branch of the Fox River crosses under the highway. We'll cross it again when we head up 77 toward Grand Marais." He looks at him. "That's a good trout stream if you ever get up to the cabin in the future. Probably won't have time to fish it this trip."

Robby's eyes go from his grandfather's face to the little bridge in the distance. He shrugs. "Maybe you and I could come up another time and fish it. I'd do that."

Otto stares down the highway. Then he turns to Robby and holds out his hand. "Give me the keys."

Robby pauses a moment and then reaches into his pocket. He sets the keys in his waiting palm.

Otto nods to the other side of the car. "Go buckle yourself in."

Robby goes to the passenger side and gets in. Otto adjusts himself in the driver's seat. Sticking the key in the ignition, he turns the engine over. It grumbles, idling. He checks in the rearview mirror and then looks ahead into the empty highway.

He clicks his seat belt. "So you actually going to drive it this time?"

Otto pulls the lever into *drive* and then jams his foot down on the gas. The tires spit up gravel and a cloud of dust.

The takeoff presses Robby back against his seat. "Jesus Christ, Grandpa."

"Just hang on." He pulls them onto the asphalt and holds the wheel steady. The needle climbs swiftly up the speedometer and is at 60 mph by the time they shoot over the bridge.

Two fishermen in a canoe turn to watch them rocket past.

After another couple hundred feet, the Firebird is going 80 mph. They are pushing past 90 when they meet the first car coming in the opposite direction. Robby grips the seat and checks the passing car. It's not police.

Otto glances at Robby and then back to the road. "This sonuvabitch has some giddy-up in her, doesn't she, boy?"

Robby nods. The scrubland outside his window blurs past. He huffs out a small laugh.

"Here we go," Otto shouts, laughing out loud. The needle climbs over 100 mph. He eases the wheel to the right as the road gradually curves.

"Grandpa, you should probably—"

"I got this, boy. Don't you worry."

Another car flashes past in the opposite lane, the sound of it doppling and then instantly disappearing.

"God damn, we're moving!"

The speedometer reads 115 mph. The road hooks gradually to the left and soon after begins a longer curve to the right. Gripping the wheel in both hands, Otto eases the car along the route effortlessly.

Robby looks over at his grandfather's smiling face. He shakes his head and laughs out a smile of his own.

A moment later, Otto lets off the gas. The speedometer slides down...100, 95, 90, 85, 80...

They are going 60 when they shimmy over a set of railroad tracks. The road curves to the left just after. When they are out of the curve and the road straightens again, the outlying homes on the east side of a small village appear on either side of the road. Otto backs the car off to 45 mph. "Seney," he says.

Robby studies the landscape slowing around them. "What the

hell was that, Grandpa?" He laughs. "Trying to make up lost time or what?"

Otto hits the turn signal and pulls the car up to the pumps at the Oasis Fuel gas station. He cuts the engine and sits with his swollen hands on the wheel. He sighs. "Just wanted to do that one time," he says. "I'd never really opened her up like that."

"She sure moves." Robby looks out the window at a real estate sign in front of the gas station. "I think this place is closed, Grandpa."

Otto opens his door. "It's all yours," he says, leaving the keys dangling in the ignition. "I'm done." He walks not around to the passenger door, but instead away from the car. His gait is rigid and resolute. He steps between two rust-stained gas pumps and toward the entrance of the abandoned gas station.

Robby watches him through the windshield.

~*~

Robby sits on a metal folding chair. Picking up the staple gun from the table next to him, he looks around the interior of the screened-in porch. The land around the cabin is grown up with mainly cedar and birch. Just down the porch steps, a sandy trail leads away to the north through the trees.

He studies the silver of the staple gun a moment and then sets it back on the table. He reaches down into his pocket.

Otto comes out of the cabin door and stands with his hands on his hips. He wears jeans and a flannel shirt. He looks around the porch. "All done?"

Robby nods, jerking his hand from his pocket. "Just finished." He scratches his arm. "And that bug spray you gave me didn't do anything. I think it was like barbecue sauce for them."

Otto walks up close to one of the screens. "I told you to wear long sleeves." He presses his hand against the mesh. "Good. Nice and tight." He looks at Robby. "Good job."

"Thanks." He crosses his arms and squeezes them against his chest. "Do you really think it was a bear?"

Otto touches the screen again. "Could have been a raccoon or a bird. Sometimes a bird will fly through it, and if it's still alive can fly back out. Whatever it was, it was a helluva a hole." He walks over and sits in the table's other folding chair. He looks at his hands and opens and closes his enflamed fingers. "Looks like all that work was for nothing."

"What time is it?"

"After four."

Robby looks out the screen toward the trees. "Still pretty early—"

"They'd be here by now if they were coming."

A mosquito hovers over Robby's wrist and then lands. He smacks it. Lifting his hand, he reveals a smear of blood.

Otto looks. "Got the bastard, eh?"

He wipes his wrist on his pants. "Uncle Jack might have gotten a late start."

Otto picks up the hammer from the table and turns it back and forth. "I don't know. I doubt it. More likely, he's three sheets to the wind somewhere." He sets the hammer down. "I don't even know why I thought they would come."

Robby looks at the hammer. "Why did you want them to come, Grandpa?"

"What?"

"What did you want to do if they came up here?"

Otto stands up and goes into the camp. When he comes out again a moment later, he sets two open beer bottles on the table. "You like Killians? I've never had it, but I heard that it's good." He takes a drink and then sets the bottle on the table. "Hmm, it is good. Nothing like a beer after doing some hard work, right?"

Robby stares at him. "Grandpa, you don't drink."

He takes another sip of his beer. "It's been almost thirty years. I think I can handle one."

Robby touches his fingers along his bottle. "I don't think any of my counselors would agree with you."

"They'd be right, too."

He rubs his palm over his forehead. "I really don't think—"

"I was a rat bastard to those boys. A real piece of shit." He sets his fist tapping against his lips. "I just wanted a chance to really apologize to them one more time. I wanted to hear them really forgive me."

Robby picks up his bottle. They sit for a moment taking sips.

"I went to the hospital when my old man was dying," Otto says. "He called the house and asked if I'd come see him." He takes a drink and then sets down the bottle. "I wasn't going to go, but your grandmother made me." He shakes his head. "Jesus Christ, she was a good woman. I look back and can't figure out why she ever stayed with me. I gave her plenty reasons to leave." He looks at Robby and smiles. "If you can, boy, marry a Catholic. All that guilt gives them a lot of resilience."

Robby sips his beer. "What did your dad say when you went to see him?"

Otto looks out the screen into the trees. "That sonuvabitch used to really beat the hell out of me. No reason, he'd come into my bedroom and just start swinging. I tried locking the door, but that would just piss him off more. Kicked the door in once so bad that I couldn't even close it anymore." He takes another drink. "Once or twice a month he'd turn me into a punching bag. Then a lot of months would pass where he wouldn't. Went on like that for years until I was old enough to get out of there."

Robby looks into his lap. "Your mom didn't do anything?"

"She was dead. She died giving birth to my brother. They both died." He takes a drink. "Probably why dad was so angry."

Robby looks up and out toward the trees. "My dad told me that things were really tough for you when you were—"

"My old man started crying when I walked into that hospital room. Just sobbing." He points his finger at Robby. "He didn't even need to say anything. That was him apologizing right there. Just him crying was all I needed to see." Otto wipes his fingers under his eye. "I went and sat on the edge of his bed and lifted him up to me and just hugged him. I held him for a long time. He died two days later."

Robby sits, absently holding his bottle.

"I quit drinking right after my dad died. Well, I quit drinking a few times. Cold turkey didn't work, so your grandmother got me into a program. That worked." He holds his beer bottle in front of him and studies the label. "Your dad...he got the good me. I'm sure that made the other boys bitter. I know it did for Jacky. I tried a lot of times to talk to them. I wanted to try to make things right with them…be a decent dad for them, too, I guess." He shakes his head. "They wanted nothing to do with me. I lived with that. I didn't have much other choice." He stares out the screen. "A man shouldn't have to live forever accounting for what he did in the past. That's not right."

He stands up and walks toward the screen door. "A man has to be forgiven, I think, if he's really sorry and the things happened a long time ago. That's all I wanted to have happen up here this weekend. Just some closure."

Holding his beer, he walks through the screen door, down the steps, and onto the sandy trail.

Robby watches him go. "Grandpa?"

He keeps walking and disappears into the trees.

Following the trail, Robby comes out of the trees. Ahead of him rises a hill of sugar sand. Clumps of champlain beachgrass ripple in the wind. He follows his grandfather's footprints up and, at its crest, the dune looks out onto the blue expanse of Lake Superior as far as he can see to the north, east, and west. The surface undulates in the distance and breaks into slow-rolling whitecaps near the shore. The water is a study in blues. The whisper of the waves fills the air, shushing everything.

His grandfather stands near the shore looking out over the water. His beer bottle dangles from the tips of his fingers. Robby walks up and stands next to him. They watch the water for a moment together.

"I don't know that you're right, Grandpa."

"What?"

Robby doesn't turn from the water. "Not everyone gets forgiven. Sometimes whatever was done was so bad, it's not enough to be sorry. Nobody owes you forgiveness."

Otto rubs his fingertips into his eyes.

Robby reaches down into his pocket and pulls out the little pill bottle.

Otto looks at the container and makes a noise in his throat. "I thought you might still be using that shit," he mumbles.

"I'm not," Robby says. "I've had this with me ever since I got out of rehab. I figured that was the only way to really test myself. I've been tempted a few times, but I never took any." He opens the bottle and lets five pills fall into the wet sand. He grinds them down with the heel of his shoe. "I think I'm officially clean or damn close to it."

Otto puts his hand on Robby's back and rubs a circle there. Then, he lifts his beer bottle, looks at it, and dumps the remainder into the sand. "T.I.A." he says.

Robby looks at the Rorschach of beer-soaked sand. "What?"

"Back on the Au Sable. That's what happened to me. A transient ischemic attack. It's like a mini-stroke. That was my third."

Robby looks out at the lake. In the distance, a smudge of iron ore freighter sits on top of the water. "What does that mean?"

"It means I'm not going back with you."

Robby snaps his head towards him. "What does that mean?"

"Just what I said. I'm not going back. You'll take the car and head home tomorrow."

Robby blinks back tears. "Grandpa..."

"It's my carotid arteries...in my neck. You know them?"

He shakes his head.

"Main supply of blood to the brain. Shit, I don't know much about them myself other than doctors telling me 50 ways to Sunday what's wrong with mine." He scratches some fingers into his hair. "The one on the left side of my neck is blocked 70 percent, and the one on my right is completely blocked. Surgery's risky because of some other health issues I have. Little stuff, but they complicate things. Either way, surgery or not, there's a good chance that I have a major stroke in my future. A real good chance."

Robby stares out at the freighter. He clicks a fingernail against the spaces between a couple molars.

"I have a friend who had a major stroke," Otto says. "He didn't die from it, though. They got him to the hospital in time so the bastards could save him, which was about the cruelest thing that I've seen done to someone. There's barely anything left of him. If that happened to me I'd want to kill myself." He shakes his head. "That poor sonuvabitch couldn't kill himself now even if you set a loaded gun on a table in front of him."

He looks at his grandfather's resolved profile staring out at the endless water.

"I'm not waiting for that to happen to me. No way."

A tear slides down Robby's cheek.

"I've got some paperwork for you up in the camp. You're getting everything. If you end up wanting to split some of it with your uncles, that's up to you. I would have made some changes to the paperwork had they come up here, but they didn't. What it comes down to is pretty much the house, everything that's in it, the cars, and about thirty-two thousand dollars I have in savings. Taught myself to live pretty thin over the years, probably too thin, so I was able to get by with just what Social Security sent me."

More tears stream down Robby's face. "Grandpa, I don't want your stuff."

"Don't have a lot of choice, boy. It's yours. Just think about what you could do with that money. Plus, if you don't think you want to live in the house, you could sell it. Probably clear close to a hundred thousand. You could go to school or do whatever. You should definitely sell the car. No reason to hang on to a relic like that."

He drops the beer bottle in the sand. "Bring that up with you when you come up, will ya? I'm going to go start the steaks."

"Grandpa..."

Otto trudges over the sand back toward the cabin. "Thanks for driving me up here and everything. That means a lot."

Robby turns back toward the enormity of the lake. He wipes the back of his hand under his eyes.

~*~

Robby sits on the beach, twisting the bottom of the beer bottle back and forth into the sand. He watches his hand do it, looks out at the water, and then watches his hand again. His eyes are red and swollen. The waves whisper along the shoreline. He looks behind him at his grandfather's footprints going up and out of sight over the small dune of sand.

He startles when his cell phone rings. He takes it out of his pocket and looks at the screen.

Tif

He answers.

"I saw that you called a couple times," she says.

He stands up. "I did." He paces down the shore. "I'm glad that you called back."

"Sorry it…ile…"

He switches the phone to his other ear. "You're breaking up a little bit. I'm way up here on the beach by Lake Superior. What did you say?"

"I said sorry that it took me awhile to get back to you."

He walks back to where he was standing when the phone rang. "No problem. I know you're busy with everything."

"What are you doing by Lake Superior?"

He looks to the west. The gold of the beach and the blue of the water stretch side by side curving into the distance. "That's where my grandpa's place is. Practically right on the water."

"Must be beautiful."

He looks out at the water, endless to the northern horizon. The freighter is gone. "It's not bad, that's for sure."

She clears her throat. "Why did you call?"

"What?"

"When you called from the road…why did you call me?"

He shrugs. "Just to talk."

She's quiet a moment. "I'm not moving back into my mom's place."

"You're not?"

"No. I found a place that I can move into next week. I'm pretty sure that I'll be able to afford it."

He switches the phone again. "I'd like to help."

"Robby…"

"I mean with moving you in…you know, if you need the help."

"I'd like that."

He crouches down and runs his palm over the smooth, wet sand near the water. "What if, though?"

"What if, what?"

He scoops out a handful of muddy sand and holds it in his palm. The hole left behind begins to fill with water. "What if I wanted to do more than just help you move?"

"Robby, I don't know..."

He drops the sand. "I'll take that." Standing up, he slaps his palm against his pant leg. "I'll take 'I don't know.'"

"Robby—"

"We can end it there, right? Let's just end it with 'I don't know' for now. That'd be good, I think."

She takes a long breath and exhales. "Okay."

He closes his eyes and puts his head back, smiling. "I'll call you then when I get back into town."

"Okay," she says. "I'm still going to hold you to helping me move."

"I'll be there."

"Okay. Then I'll talk to you soon."

"Sounds good, Tif."

They hang up. Robby holds the phone in his hand and stares out at the expanse of water.

Otto walks up behind him and sets his arm around his shoulders. "The coals are hot, boy. I'm going to throw the steaks on pretty soon. They won't take long. You coming up?"

He nods. "I'll be up in a minute."

Otto rubs his hand up and down Robby's back before turning away.

"Grandpa?"

"Yeah?"

He turns and faces him. "I probably won't sell the car right away. It's kind of grown on me."

He smiles. "That's fine. I like the idea that you'll keep it around for a while." He takes a few steps, bends over, and picks up his beer bottle.

~*~

Robby takes a deep breath and then looks down at his phone. He has a single bar of connection. He opens his contacts, slides his finger down the screen, and then hits send.

"Hello?"

"Hi, Mrs. Sanders. It's Robby Cooper."

"Robby Cooper? Oh my God. I haven't heard your voice in such a long time."

He pushes his hand through his hair. "It's been awhile." He sniffs in a breath. "Actually, I was calling to talk to Duffy."

"You're breaking up, honey."

He takes a few steps backwards. "Is that better?"

"Yes."

"I wanted to know if Duffy is home."

"No, David's not here. He's—"

"Is he still in seminary?"

"No."

"Oh." He looks down at the sand. "I really thought that he was going to—"

She laughs. "Robby, David is in his pastoral placement at St. Fabians in Farmington Hills. He'll be a priest in a year or two."

He looks up from the sand to the endless blue water. He smiles. "Really?" he says. "That's great to hear. That's really great."

~*~

Robby slides his finger through his contacts and stops on *Mom*. After a moment, he presses her number and her phone begins to ring.

"Since when do you not answer your phone," he says to the voice mail system. "Anyway, I'm calling to check in. I'm doing okay."

The waves continue at the shoreline, pulling some grains of sand away and setting others back.

~*~

Robby idles the Firebird outside the gated parking lot of a moving company on Jefferson Ct. in Detroit. Across the street, a vacant lot is overgrown with long, yellowed grass and weeds. Trees and bushes that haven't been cut back in years grow chokingly into the cyclone fence that runs the perimeter of the lot.

He shifts into *park* and presses the gas pedal. The engine revs a crescendoed growl into the air above the dead end street.

After a moment, the door to the moving company opens. A tall, thin black man emerges and shuffles toward the gate, followed by a wiry pit bull mix. The man's low-cut afro is wisped throughout with mists of gray hair. Watching the Firebird, he undoes a padlocked chain, and then slowly pulls open the chain-link gate. He waves Robby in.

Robby pulls the car in between the faded yellow lines of a parking space near the door of the building. He cuts the engine.

The other man walks the gate back into its place. Watching Robby get out of the car, he pulls a pack of cigarettes from a front pocket. The dog sits down a few feet from the man and watches Robby.

The man flicks a flame up to his smoke. "That's a car there," he says. "They don' make 'em like that no more."

Robby closes the door and nods. Then, he swallows. "Is he inside?"

Cigarette fit between his lips, the man bends down for the chain and begins threading it back through the gate and the adjoining section of fence. "He is," he says. "He's waitin' on you."

Robby watches the man's thin fingers snapping the padlock back into place. He touches his pant pocket, pats it.

~*~

Andre's office is small and consumed by a huge metal desk and metal filing cabinets. A calendar some five years out of date hangs beneath the picture of a smiling naked woman. Sitting in an ashtray on the faded and cracked blotter, a smoldering cigarette sends up a thin string of smoke. A ceiling fan circles slowly overhead.

On the phone, Andre glances at Robby and then motions to a visitor's chair on the other side of the desk. Robby sits.

Andre squeezes his hand on top of his bald head. "What the fuck am I, Mapquest? Jesus. You're telling me you guys can't find the house?" He shakes his head. "Couple a rocket scientists. And what the hell are you calling me for? You got the number, call the goddamn homeowner, for Christ's sake."

Robby scratches his arm and looks at the floor.

"I don't care if you're doing it in the dark. I want that place packed up today and the shit delivered to the new place. You hearing me?" He listens a moment. "Okay," he says and hangs up.

Robby looks up and nods. "Andre."

Andre takes a pack of cigarettes from the desk and shakes one up. He pulls it out with his teeth. He smiles around the cigarette. "I should call one of them ghost shows. I think I got a goddamn ghost sitting right here in my office."

Robby sets an envelope on the desk. "I got it with me. All of it."

Andre lights his smoke. "Almost 11 months without my money, what do you want me to do…thank you?"

Robby sets his hands in his lap. "No."

Andre reaches out and pulls the envelope toward him.

"It's all there," Robby says. "Ten thousand. You can count it—"

"Don't tell me my business. And don't say ten thousand like it's some huge amount. It's a fucking gift is what it is. Three thousand dollars with a 20 point vig? Bi-weekly? You don't even want to know how much you really owe me."

Robby looks at the floor again.

Andre takes a drag and blows the smoke toward the fan blades.

The door to the building opens and the man from outside walks past the office door with the dog trailing behind him.

"You feed him?" Andre asks, raising his voice.

A moment passes. "Yeah."

A smile nicks Andre's face. "Willie?"

"Alright. Alright. I was jus' about to. Can't do something on time if you always asking me if it's done already."

Andre shakes his head and looks at Robby. "I'm too soft. Mother fuckers walking all over me."

Robby looks up and then down again. He clears his throat. "You didn't do anything."

"What?"

"To my mom or Tiffany...when I didn't get you the money."

Andre leans forward and mashes the cigarette into the ashtray, simultaneously snuffing out the other smouldering cigarette. "I got eyes and ears out there. I knew about your grandpa's funeral. Gave you a little grace period, especially when I heard you were selling his house. Figured you were squaring up your shit."

Robby nods. "Thanks."

Andre leans back in his chair. "Now get the fuck out of here. I don't ever want to see your sorry ass again."

Robby stands up. "Sorry about everything, Andre. I really am."

Andre reaches for his cigarettes. He smiles. "You're forgiven, shithead. Just remember, if you ever need money again, I'll kick your ass to the curb if you come sniffing around here."

"I won't."

Robby stands at the driver's side of the Firebird. He reaches into his back pocket. Taking out a folded piece of paper, he unfolds it and smooths it on the car's roof. He fishes a stub of pencil from his back pocket.

Willie opens the door to the building and steps out onto the stoop. He moves slowly down the steps, watching Robby.

"What you got there...grocery list?"

Robby looks at him and smiles. "Nah."

Willie studies him a moment and then shuffles toward the gate. "Well, keep your secrets then. I'll let you outta here."

"Thanks."

Underneath the words *talked with Duffy*, Robby writes *paid off Andre*. He looks over the list for a moment before folding it and stuffing it and the pencil back into his pocket. Behind him, the padlock snaps open. The chain jangle-slides through the links.

Willie walks the gate open.

Robby gets in the Firebird, rolls down the window, and then turns over the engine.

"Damn boy," Willie shouts over the noise, "that sounds fine!"

Robby smiles at him.

~*~

Robby turns right onto East Jefferson Ave. In the distance, buildings in the downtown jut up over the horizon. The asphalt ahead of him is dull gray and splitting. The buildings along the roadside are a mix of closed businesses, liquor stores, dated motels, and newer pop-up banks, pharmacies, and dollar stores. A sign on the side of a brick building reads *T-Mobile Loves Detroit*. On his left, an old water tower looms over a three-story warehouse. The only activity in the building is an open-pit barbecue joint and a bible bookstore. A few people on the sidewalk glance toward the Firebird as it grumbles past.

~*~

The buildings of the Ren Cen shoot up into the sky on his left. Here the city appears as any other metropolis. Business people with laptop computer cases or briefcases hustle along the sidewalk. A police car idles on either side of him at a stop light. And then, on his left, suspended from a tri-pod like the heart of the city in a rib-cage, the colossal replica of Joe Lewis' fist. Not far away from it, a man or a woman, gender lost in layers of ratty clothes, sits leaning against a lamp post. Robby turns the car up onto Woodward Ave.

~*~

He races out of the financial district, out of the shadows of the skyscrapers, past Grand Circus Park, and the baseball stadium, the Fox Theatre and then across the Fisher Freeway, past the D.S.O., Wayne State's campus, the D.I.A., the Detroit Public Library, and then over the Edsel Ford Freeway, where Woodward becomes something that the city has been trying to hide. All the glass of storefronts is covered in a tight mesh of steel and iron gates. Business are closed. Everything locks. Cigarettes are sold in singles out of bullet proof windows. The pedestrians shamble or sit, stand or lean—their faces vacant, desperate, hungry or angry—looking lost as though something was taken from them.

Robby pats his hand over the bulge in his pocket.

~*~

Near the Fisher Theater, construction vehicles surround an Art Deco apartment building. Four men up on scaffolding fit a new pane of glass into the window above the building's foyer.

~*~

Turning off of West Grand Boulevard, Robby descends from the service drive down to the Lodge Freeway. He rubs his hand over his forehead. The Firebird flickers out of the light into the shadow of overpasses and then back into the light. On the right of the highway, above him past cyclone fencing, houses and buildings gape with smashed out windows. Whole houses partially burned open through walls or through roofs have not been demolished. From the gutters, small shafts of saplings grow up from the sludge there. What once were homes are framed in charred wood with foundations of ash. He glances at them and then back to the road ahead.

~*~

Fishing down into his pocket, he pulls out the small shape of plastic and turns it in his hand.

A pacifier. He looks at it and smiles.

He tilts the rearview mirror down until the tiny car seat strapped in the back is reflected there. He smiles again, tossing the pacifier over his shoulder and watching it land in the seat. He tilts the mirror back up, sees the city skyline towering in the distance behind him, and then turns on the radio.

Rush's "Tom Sawyer" resounds out of the speakers. Like hummingbird wings, Robby's fingers strum Geddy Lee's bass line on the edge of the steering wheel. Two of his knuckles are flecked with dried green paint. He pushes the Firebird up to 80 and threads his way through the traffic, rising up the freeway, like mercury.